KT-479-996

BEST FRIENDS'
Bakery

A Spoonful of Secrets

Cardiff Libraries
www.cardiff.gov.uk/libraries

Llyfrgelloedd Caerdydd
www.caerdydd.gov.uk/llyfrgelloedd

CARDIFF
CAERDYDD

WH

ACC. No: 03217116
CDF

Also by Linda Chapman

BEST FRIENDS' BAKERY

Sugar and Spice

A Spoonful of Secrets

LINDA CHAPMAN

Illustrated by Kate Hindley

Orion
Children's Books

First published in Great Britain 2014
by Orion Children's Books
a division of the Orion Publishing Group Ltd
Orion House
5 Upper St Martin's Lane
London WC2 9EA
An Hachette UK company

1 3 5 7 9 10 8 6 4 2

Text © Linda Chapman 2014
Illustrations © Kate Hindley 2014

The right of Linda Chapman and Kate Hindley
to be identified as the author and illustrator respectively
of this work has been asserted.

All rights reserved. No part of this publication may be
reproduced, stored in a retrieval system, or transmitted,
in any form or by any means, electronic, mechanical,
photocopying, recording or otherwise, without the
prior permission of the Orion Publishing Group.

The Orion Publishing Group's policy is to use papers
that are natural, renewable and recyclable products and
made from wood grown in sustainable forests. The logging
and manufacturing processes are expected to conform to
the environmental regulations of the country of origin.

A catalogue record for this book is
available from the British Library.

Printed in Great Britain

ISBN 978 1 4440 1190 6

www.orionbooks.co.uk

To Iola, Jess D, Poppy, Anna,
Georgia P, Lucy, Jess J, Georgia S,
Phoebe S, Ellenoor and Hannah, who have all
tried out the recipes or answered
endless questions. Thank you!

MY BAKING BOOK (and other stuff)

Hi, I'm Hannah.

Age: 10 3/4

Birthday: 1st August

Likes: baking, drawing, swimming, seeing my friends

Dislikes: spiders and slugs

This is my journal. It's for all sorts of important things - lists, cake designs, cookery facts, a few other things, but most of all for RECIPES!

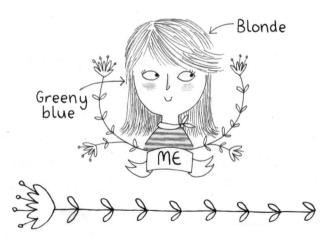

Blonde

Greeny blue

ME

1

SUGAR & SPICE
BAKERY
↖ the <u>BEST</u> bakery
in the <u>WORLD</u>!

Do you know the saying, Don't just dream it – do it? It's one of my favourite sayings. Having dreams is good, but making them come true is even better.

My mum used to dream of opening a bakery, and now she has. It's called the Sugar and Spice Bakery. It's only been open for ten days and it's perfect. It's in an old building in a town called Ashingham on a quiet side street just out of the town centre. It has a door with a bell that tinkles as you walk in, shelves filled with every kind of cake, pastry and bread you can think of, and the wonderful smell of fresh baking just pulls you inside. It's officially my favourite place in the world.

Mum does all the baking on her own at the moment, but she's got an apprentice starting next week. He's called Dylan – he's eighteen and wants to be a baker. I haven't met him yet. I try to help Mum when I can, though I'm at school most days (obviously), so usually I just help when she's working in the evenings, like when she's making the special celebration cakes that people order.

When I'm at the bakery, I work behind the counter with Paula. I'm not old enough to work properly, so I just do as much as I'm allowed. I ask the customers what they want and wrap their cakes and pastries. Paula's in her fifties (Mum says) and she's really nice. She knows nearly everyone in Ashingham. If she were a cake or a pastry, I think she'd be something like a fruit scone – small, round, warm and friendly.

Sorry – I guess that sounds a bit weird, but I have this thing where I always compare the people I know to bakery things. My mum's a hot cross bun: a mixture of sugar and spice, sweet and kind but also a bit stubborn and with a temper.

We've just moved here, so until last week I'd been dreading starting my new school. In Ashingham, if you're in Year 6, you go to something called a middle school. It's much bigger than a normal primary school, more like a secondary school, because it has Years 5, 6, 7 and 8. I was really worried at first that I'd get lost and that I wouldn't make any friends because I was starting halfway through the school year. Luckily, before I started school, I met Alice, Misha, Lara and Mia who are all in Year 6 too. We went to school together on Monday – three days ago – and I've been hanging round with them every day.

Misha is the loud one of our group: she's always calling out in class, but she's clever so the teachers let her get away with it. She's like a 'look at me' strawberry tart, bursting with jam and strawberries, who

everyone notices. She loves dancing and singing and ponies.

Alice and Lara like ponies too. Lara is a bit quieter than Misha. She's more of a blueberry muffin – popular but not attention-grabbing. Alice is cheerful and friendly and very pretty. She reminds me of an iced cupcake with

sugar flowers on the top – the sort of cake everyone likes.

And then there's Mia. Even though she's not in the same class as me and the others, she's my best, best friend in Ashingham

– we're both baking-
mad! Mia's gran
taught her to bake
and she loves
coming to the
bakery. When
we're older we're
going to open our own
bakery. And share a
house and have a dog and a
cat. That's a dream I REALLY want to make
come true!

It took me a while to decide what sort of bake Mia would be, but finally I worked out she'd be a loaf of Mum's sourdough bread. At first it's easy to overlook her because she's quiet, but when you get to know her you realise she's one of the nicest people ever – just like freshly-baked sourdough bread is one of the nicest types of bread. It's soft and chewy in the middle and crunchy on the outside. Yum! Mia's funny and loyal and I never have to worry that I'm talking too much about baking when I'm with her. She's quite shy, though, and until I came along she said she didn't really have any friends at school.

Also, the Year Seven girl who used to bully her, Tegan McGarrity, has left her alone so far this term, which is really good.

Tomorrow, Mia and I are going to the new Baking Club at lunchtime. I'm hoping we'll get to do something fun. Fingers crossed!

So, that's my life. The bakery, school, my friends and family. Welcome to my world!

2

"So, you're off to Baking Club tomorrow," my mum said, getting a pie plate out of the cupboard as I rubbed butter into flour, salt and icing sugar to make a sweet shortcrust pastry dough. We were making an apple and cinnamon pie to have after dinner. For the first week of the bakery being open, Mum was too tired to do any baking at home, but last weekend she'd announced she was going to make more of an effort from now on. I was really pleased – I love baking with Mum. "Do you know anyone who goes already?"

"No," I said, as the flour and butter gradually changed to breadcrumbs between my fingers and thumbs. "Mia hasn't been

before, because she didn't want
to go on her own. And Misha,
Alice and Lara think it's lame."

Mum glanced at me, a smudge
of flour on her cheek. Her blonde hair, the
same colour as mine, was tied back in a messy
bun. "And you're still going?"

"Of course," I said. I know some people
find it hard to do things if their friends tease
them, but I'm not like that. I've always
thought that if your friends are really your
friends they'll like you no matter what.

Mum blew me a kiss. "That's my girl. Do
what *you* want, not what others think you
should do. I'd never have opened this bakery
if I'd listened to everyone who told me it was
mad. You and Mark were the only people
who believed in me."

Mark's my step-dad. My mum and dad
split up when I was two, and Dad went to
live in America. I haven't seen Dad for over
a year. We Skype each other sometimes and
he always remembers my birthday or when
I have something important coming up, but

Mark's the one who's around all the time. I like him. He's a freshly-baked granary loaf – strong, kind, reliable and comforting.

He and Mum got married a few weeks ago and we all moved in together – me, Mum, Mark, and Molly and Ella, Mark's four-year-old twin daughters. It's strange having little sisters after having been just me and Mum for so long. I'm getting used to it, though. They can be really cute at times, but I REALLY wish they wouldn't jump on my bed at six o'clock every morning!

Mum started adding some beaten eggs to the butter and flour mixture, gently working it in with a knife, then bringing it together into a ball with her hands. She patted it into a flat round shape. Then I dusted it with flour, wrapped it in cling film, and put it in the fridge to rest.

MY TOP TIPS FOR MAKING SWEET SHORTCRUST PASTRY:

1. Use icing sugar not caster sugar
2. Run your hands under a cold tap first so they are cold when you start rubbing the butter into the flour and sugar.
3. Try to handle the pastry as little as possible. Use a cold knife to mix the eggs in before bringing it together in a ball with your hands.
4. Wrap the pastry in clingfilm and leave in the fridge for at least 20 minutes before rolling it out.

I love making pastry. It's one of my favourite things to bake.

"It's weird how lots of different types of pastry are made from the same basic ingredients but they all turn out so differently, isn't it?" I said to Mum. "I mean, sweet shortcrust and choux pastry have

11

almost exactly the same things in them, but they're completely different when they're baked. And puff pastry and normal shortcrust are made from the same things, and they're very different too."

"Pastry *is* magical," agreed Mum. "And what's brilliant is that each pastry is right for the job it does. A fruit pie wouldn't work with a choux topping, and you couldn't make a profiterole out of shortcrust pastry."

"You know what I'd really like to learn to make?" I said. "Danish pastries."

"We've made Danishes together before," said Mum, in surprise.

"I know, but you've always made the dough in advance. I'd like to learn how to make them from the start."

"Well, that shouldn't be too hard," Mum said. "The dough takes a long time to prove but we could start it on Saturday night. I have to go into the bakery on Sunday morning to make a wedding cake so we could finish the Danishes then."

"I'd love that!" I said. "Can I ask Mia?"

"Of course," said Mum. "But for now . . ." She looked at the pie filling, cooling on the hob. "Time to finish this pie."

We rolled out the pastry and lined the pie plate, brushing egg white on the bottom and then sprinkling semolina over it to stop the bottom of the pie getting soggy with the fruit juices.

"Was the bakery busy again today?" I asked as Mum spooned in the filling.

"It was!" she said happily. "We sold out of bread, and all the breakfast pastries went too. Once Dylan starts, I'll have to get him making more of everything through the day. Word seems to be getting around about us."

I felt very relieved. When Mum opened, the bakery had been really quiet, and for the first week we'd worried it was going to be a total flop. Then I'd come up with the idea of giving out free samples at the local farmers' market and we'd held a charity bake sale for Paula's nephew, Tom, who was really ill and needed to go to America for an operation. Since then,

Mum had more and more customers coming to the bakery every day.

"Now, all I want is a few more orders for birthday cakes and special occasion cakes," Mum said. "They're great fun to do."

Mum is brilliant at making big special occasion cakes. She loves all the decorating and getting everything just perfect, making each cake individual and unique.

"I had another order today," Mum went on. "It was from Sarah – you know, the lady who comes into the bakery with the son who plays tennis."

I knew who she meant. They came into the bakery quite often, on their way to or from the boy's tennis lessons. I didn't like him. He looked about eleven or twelve and always seemed to be in a bad mood. I'd tried saying hello to him a few times but he just ignored me. He seemed really rude.

"He's called George, isn't he?" I said.

"That's right. George King. Apparently he's just won a big junior tennis tournament and Sarah wants a cake for a party they're having

to celebrate on Saturday.
I've never made a cake
with a tennis theme before."
A new cake! Exciting! "Maybe
you could do it in the
shape of a tennis racquet or a

tennis ball. Or a tennis court
with a net and a tennis player
holding a trophy, or

a tiered cake with tennis
balls on," I said.
Mum looked
thoughtful. "I do like
the tennis court idea. I
could make the tennis player
look like George. I'll see what his
mum thinks tomorrow. I said I'd
have some designs done by then.
She seems very nice. George
isn't at your school, is he?"

I shook my head. When
he'd first come in during the
holidays, he had always been in
his tennis gear, but the last few days

he'd been in the blue-and-gold uniform that the boys from Ashingham School, the boys-only private school a few miles away, wore.

"I'll probably make the cake on Friday evening – do you want to help?" Mum said.

"Yes, please." Any chance to bake with Mum was fine by me!

We finished the pie, decorating the top with some little cut-out apple shapes made out of leftover pastry.

"All ready to go," said Mum, popping it into the oven.

We were just in time. There was the sound of a key in the front door and voices in the hall, as Mark and the twins came home. The twins had been at their childminder's. Mark picked them up on his way home from work.

They ran in, with Mark following behind, carrying their bags and lunchboxes.

"What's for tea?" said Ella.

"I'm hungry!" said Molly.

"Nice to see you too, girls," said Mum, with a smile.

They came over and gave her a hug.

Molly's a pink meringue – girly and very sweet.

Ella's a chocolate brownie – easy to like and bouncy

MOLLY

ELLA

"It smells good in here," said Mark, sniffing appreciatively. The sweet, spicy smell of apple and cinnamon scented the air. "Apple pie?"

"Yep," said Mum. "Homemade chicken burgers first and apple pie for pudding."

"Delicious," said Mark, giving her a kiss. "How was your day, Hannah?"

"Fine, thanks."

Molly grabbed my hand. "Will you come outside with us? We're going to play princesses on the climbing frame. I'm going to be Princess Belle . . ."

"And I'm Superdog and I'm going to rescue her," said Ella.

"You're the wicked queen who's keeping me prisoner," Molly said. "You can chase us!"

"I should help tidy up," I said quickly. I didn't really feel like playing.

"No, you go," said Mum. "I'll do it."

"Please," Molly begged, staring up at me with big hazel eyes.

"Pretty please!" said Ella.

There was clearly no escape. "OK," I sighed. "But I have to do my homework, so I'm not playing for long."

The twins squealed in delight and dragged me into the garden where I spent the next half an hour pretending to be a wicked queen who chased them. It was actually quite fun, though I was VERY glad my new school friends weren't there to see me.

3

Mia called round next morning so we could walk to school together.

"Bye!" I shouted to Mark and the twins, who were in the kitchen eating their breakfast.

"Have a good day," Mark called back. Mum had already gone to the bakery – she starts at five o'clock every day.

I joined Mia outside. Her straight, shoulder-length strawberry blonde hair was tied back in a low ponytail. Mia always looks neat and tidy. Unlike most of the other girls at school, her school skirt comes down to her knees and she carries a plain black rucksack rather than a flashy leather handbag. Mia's not like everyone else, though, which is one of the things I love about her.

"Is Alice walking with us today?" Mia asked.

Alice's gran, Mrs Rees, is our next-door neighbour and sometimes Alice gets dropped off at her house before school. "Not today," I said. "She texted to say Mrs Rees has to pick up one of her dogs from the vet's first thing."

"Is he OK?" Mia asked.

"He's hurt his leg, but Alice said he's going to be fine." I turned the conversation round to something I was far more interested in. "So, Baking Club today?"

Mia's eyes shone. "I'm really looking forward to it. The teacher, Miss Harris, is really nice. I wonder what we'll make."

Excitement bubbled up inside me. Going to Baking Club would be far more fun than just hanging round in the classroom chatting, which was all we usually did at lunchtime. We'd been told that school would provide the ingredients and we just needed to bring in a cake tin to take whatever we made home.

"I bet we'll do something easy for the first class," Mia went on. "Maybe cupcakes or something."

I suddenly remembered what Mum had said the night before. "Hey! Mum said she'd show us how to make Danish pastries this weekend. Do you want to come over on Saturday?"

Mia groaned. "Oh no, I can't! I'm staying at my gran and granddad's. You'll have to take pictures of all the pastries you make!"

I nodded, imagining the delicious Danish pastries. "Mmm. Flaky cinnamon whirls."

"Sticky raspberry pinwheels," said Mia.

"Chocolate chip snails," I added.

"Jam envelopes with icing sugar!" sighed Mia.

I grinned at her. When it comes to baking, sometimes it's like we speak our own secret language. I love it!

When we got to school, we fought our way through the crowds to our lockers. Misha, Lara and Alice were standing beside the Year 6 lockers. Misha was taking silly pictures on

21

her phone with a new app. The others were laughing and trying to grab the phone. Being allowed to have a mobile phone is definitely one of the best things about going to a middle school. Mum always used to say I couldn't have one until I started secondary school, but when it turned out I was going to King William's she finally gave in. I'm glad she did, or I would have been the only person without one in the entire school!

"Hey!" Misha called, spotting us. "Smile!" She held the camera up. I pulled the worst face I could, sticking my tongue out. She burst out laughing as she looked at the photo and showed it to me. It had distorted and flattened my face so that it looked as if I had three heads and six eyes.

"That looks just like you, Hannah," Alice said, grinning.

I nodded. "You've, like, totally captured my inner alien, Mish!"

Misha grinned. "Now you, Mia."

"No, don't. Please." Mia turned away quickly. "I hate having my photo taken."

Misha looked disappointed. "Don't be boring. It's fun."

Mia blushed but still hid her face. She isn't very good at being teased or laughed at.

"Take another of me," I said, pulling another face. Misha obliged.

"Hey, you've had your hair cut, Lara," I said. Lara's long blonde hair had been cut into layers. "I like it."

"It's really nice," Mia agreed.

"Thanks." Lara smiled. "I wanted it dip-dyed but my mum wouldn't let me."

"I've been trying to persuade my mum to let me have my hair dip-dyed," said Alice, sighing.

"Me too," Misha said.

Loads of the girls at school have their hair dip-dyed – it's when the end of their hair are dyed a different colour. Sometimes they dye the ends blonde, sometimes pink, sometimes even purple or green. You need long hair

Natural colour

Contrasting dyed colour

for it to look good, and pink and blonde are definitely the best colours to have.

"Mum says I have to wait until I'm at least *fourteen* before I dye my hair," said Lara. "Still, at least she let me have it cut."

"It looks really nice, Lara," said Mia. "I'd love to have long hair like yours. You're so lucky."

I winced slightly as I saw Lara blink in surprise at the gushiness of Mia's compliment. "Umm . . . thanks, Mia," she said.

I've noticed that Mia sometimes goes a bit over the top with complimenting the others and agreeing with things they say. I think it's just because she wants to fit in and be liked, but I wish she wouldn't try quite so hard. I'm sure it doesn't make the others like her more. Besides, she's brilliant just as she is.

Opening my locker, I unpacked my cake tin from my bag.

"What's that for, Hannah?" said Misha. Then she giggled. "Of course! You're going to *Baking Club* this lunchtime." She said it as if she was saying "Slug Lovers' Club". She turned to Mia. "Are you going too?"

Mia nodded.

"Mia, Mia, Mia," Misha said, sighing. "You'll really have to be cooler than this if you want to hang around with us." I knew she was only teasing, but an anxious look sprang into Mia's eyes.

"Ignore her," I said. "Baking Club is going to be great."

"It's for losers," teased Misha. "You'll smell of food all afternoon."

I grinned. "Better than smelling of horse poo! Did you wear your blazer to the stables yesterday? It smells like you did!"

Misha squawked like an outraged chicken. "It does not!"

I held my nose. "Phew! Stinky!" I said, waving a hand in front of my face.

Misha pretended to hit me. I ducked.

Alice chuckled. "Come on, you two," she said. "We should go. It'll be registration in a minute."

"Yeah, and I don't want to get into trouble for being late," said Lara.

"See you later!" I called to Mia, shutting my locker.

"Yeah, see you," she said. She looked rather wistful as I followed the others. I knew she wished she was in the same class as us.

"Baking freak," said Misha, nudging me cheerfully as we walked along.

"Pony nutter," I said, nudging her back.

We grinned at each other and went into class.

Despite what Misha had said, Baking Club was great! We made chocolate chip and fudge cookies. Miss Harris, the teacher who ran the club, was really friendly. We worked in pairs. Mia and I were together, of course. In the kitchen, Mia isn't shy at all. As she mixed the flour, salt and bicarbonate of soda in a bowl,

I started to measure out the caster sugar. Then I paused for a moment, looking at the other sugars in the glass jars on the bench.

"What are you thinking?" Mia said.

"What about swapping some of the caster sugar for muscovado sugar instead?" I said.

Mia considered. "That might work. It would go really well with the fudge and chocolate. Let's do it."

When it came to beating the sugar with the butter, we also changed the recipe a bit. Miss Harris's recipe used a lot of butter and Mia thought it might make the cookies a bit greasy.

We wondered whether to ask Miss Harris, but she was busy helping a group of Year 7s.

"Those look great, girls," Miss Harris said, coming to inspect our cookies as they cooled on the wire rack. I grinned at Mia. I had to agree. The cookies were light golden brown and the half-melted fudge and milk chocolate was oozing out. They looked light and crunchy and sticky and gooey all at the same time! Miss Harris picked one up. "Can I try?"

"Of course," I said.

Miss Harris took a bite. I felt a bit like a contestant on *Junior Brilliant Baker* as I waited to see what she thought. She nodded. A good sign. Phew!
"Mmm. These are really excellent," she said. "But this isn't my recipe – what have you done differently?"

I explained.

Miss Harris's smile grew broader. "Well, well, well. I can see I have two very serious bakers here. Well done, girls. I'm impressed!"

I felt like I was glowing.

"So, do you bake a lot at home?" Miss Harris asked.

"Yes," I said. "Actually, my mum is a baker – she's just opened a bakery in town. It's called the Sugar and Spice Bakery."

"Lucky you! Some of my friends have been and told me how good it is," Miss Harris said. "I keep meaning to pop in."

I was delighted. "I help there after school. Mia does too sometimes."

Miss Harris looked thoughtful. "You know,

28

it's just an idea, but would you two be interested in writing an article for the school magazine? There's a food section in it and someone from the Baking Club writes a feature article for each issue – I usually ask one of the older girls, but if you'd like to do it, that would be great. You could do it on whatever you like. Sometimes people just write out some of their favourite recipes; sometimes they write a piece about different things that can be baked – biscuits, pastries, pies. You can choose."

Excitement sparked inside me. Oh wow! It would be great to write a bakery article with Mia. I saw her nodding beside me. "We'd love to do it," I said.

"We'd really love to," said Mia. "When do we need to write it by?"

"The deadline is in two weeks," said Miss Harris. "Do you think you'll be able to do it by then?"

Mia and I looked at each other. "Definitely!" we chorused.

29

RECIPE FOR MINE AND MIA'S
CHOCOLATE CHIP AND FUDGE COOKIES

Ingredients:

200g plain flour

½ tsp fine salt

¼ tsp bicarbonate of soda

120g unsalted butter, at room temperature

115g caster sugar

50g muscovado sugar

1 large egg, at room temperature

1 tsp pure vanilla essence

150g milk/plain chocolate, coarsely chopped

100g fudge, coarsely chopped (you can make
   it without the fudge - just increase the
   amount of chocolate chips to 210g)

What to do:

1. Preheat the oven to 200°C.

2. Sift the flour, salt and bicarbonate of
   soda into a bowl.

3. In another bowl, beat the butter and
   both types of sugar with a hand-
   held mixer until light and fluffy. Beat
   in the egg and then the vanilla until

30

creamy. Slowly mix in the
sifted ingredients until it's
just blended and making
a soft dough. Stir in the
chopped chocolate/fudge with
a wooden spoon.

4. Line a baking tray with baking
parchment. Spoon the dough onto the
tray, leaving a good gap (about 7cm)
between the spoonfuls.

5. Bake the cookies for about 12 to 14
minutes. Leave them for a few minutes
and then move them onto a rack to
cool. Then EAT!

4

"You're doing what?" Misha spluttered, when we got back to the classroom.

"Mia and I are writing an article for the school magazine about baking," I repeated.

"That's it!" Misha declared. "You two simply cannot hang out with us any longer! No, no, no!" She put her hands up in the air dramatically and shook her head. "I'm sorry, but if you're going to do that, you'll have to find other friends."

"W-we don't have to do it." Mia glanced at me. "We could go to Miss Harris and say we've changed our minds . . ."

"Mia!" I said. "Misha's winding us up. Just ignore her."

Misha grinned and mimed winding a key at Mia.

"Oh." Mia blushed.

"It's OK," Alice said kindly. "Misha can be very convincing."

"So, what have you lot been doing that's so exciting while we've been at our losers' club?" I said, perching on one of the desks.

Lara groaned. "Getting my art homework done." She shoved her art book towards us and showed us the sketch of a rose she'd been working on.

Misha chuckled. "From this way up, it looks like a baboon's butt!"

We all giggled.

"I hope Mr Piggott doesn't think it's a baboon's butt," said Lara, turning her picture round and examining it.

"He won't – it does look like a rose the right way up," I reassured her. "Well, if you don't look at it too closely . . ."

"Of course he'll think it's a rose. I think it looks really good, Lara," Mia said sincerely.

I sighed to myself. Mia just didn't

understand the way we all joked and teased each other. It didn't mean we didn't like each other, it was just our way of being friendly.

"Thanks, Mia," Lara said. She pretended to glare at the rest of us. "At least someone's supportive!"

She and the others started packing their homework away. "So, who's going to buy Ellie B's new album tonight?" said Alice. "It was released today."

"I'm downloading it," Misha said.

"Me too," said Lara. "How about you, Hannah? Do you like Ellie B?"

"She's OK," I said. "But I'm not buying the album." I grinned cheekily. "I'll just borrow it off one of you!"

"How about you, Mia?" Alice said.

Mia froze. "Me?"

"Yeah, are you buying it?" Alice said. "Or will you scrounge it off us like Hannah?"

"Oh, yeah. Yeah, I'll buy it," said Mia, nodding. I looked at her in surprise. I knew she was even less into music than I was.

"I didn't know you liked Ellie B," Misha said.

Mia nodded. "I love her."

"So, which is your favourite song?" Lara asked.

"Um . . . favourite song? Well, it would be . . . um . . . oh, it's um . . ." Mia flushed. My heart sank. It was completely obvious that she didn't actually know any of Ellie B's songs.

"How about 'My Life'? That's my favourite," Alice said, seeming to realise the same thing and coming to Mia's rescue.

"Oh, yeah," said Mia. "'High Life', of course! That's the one."

I saw Misha and Lara glance at each other. Oh, why hadn't Mia just kept her mouth shut, or told the truth and said she wasn't that into music? No one likes fakes.

I quickly opened my cake tin to cause a distraction. "Who wants a cookie?"

The smell of freshly-baked cookies wafted out and caught everyone's attention. "Mmm, yes please!" said Alice.

I let Mia, Lara and Alice take one, then held the tin teasingly away from Misha. "You, of course, won't want something baked at rubbish old Baking Club."

"It's not rubbish. It's great!" said Misha, winking.

She took a cookie and then held up her other hand, smirking, to show me she had her fingers crossed.

Just then the bell rang for the end of lunch. Time for double maths. Mia said goodbye and left to go back to her classroom. A tiny, mean part of me felt a bit relieved. I love having her around, but sometimes it's almost painful watching her try to fit in and be liked.

I think of our group as a bit like a cake mix. I'm like the flour – I've mixed in really easily with the others – but maybe Mia is more like the eggs, and it will take a bit more mixing before she's properly part of the group. It will happen though, in time, I know it will.

Mia and I walked back to the bakery after school. Her mum has a wedding dress shop near the bakery but Mia prefers coming to help at the bakery now and she meets up with her mum later. Out of school she was back to being normal Mia again – relaxed and happy.

"I was so pleased Miss Harris liked our cookies," she said. "I can't believe she's asked us to do the article for the magazine. We'll have to think about what to write."

"Maybe we should do an article to show people like Misha that baking isn't lame," I said.

"Yeah!" said Mia. "We could put some recipes in, and lots of pictures, and show everyone how much fun it is. Maybe Misha and Lara and Alice will read it and want to come to Baking Club."

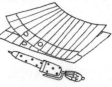

"Hmm, I don't think any article will make *that* happen!" I said. "I think we'll always be teased about Baking Club."

Mia glanced at me. "Doesn't that bother you?"

"No," I said honestly.

She heaved a sigh. "I wish I was more like you."

"What do you mean?"

"Well, you've only been at King William's for a few days and already everyone likes you."

I didn't know what to say. It was true, but to admit it seemed big-headed.

"I *never* know what to say or do," Mia went on.

"You should just be yourself," I said.

Mia looked at me as if she thought that comment wasn't very helpful. "That doesn't work. When I was myself before you came here they didn't like me."

"They just didn't know you," I said. "They do now."

Mia wasn't convinced. "I think they only let me hang round with them because of you." She looked down at her skirt, bag and shoes. "I mean, I know I don't look right, and I don't know how to join in with them when they talk and mess around."

"You'll work it out," I said. "Just relax and try to have a laugh. You can always change how you look a bit if you want. That's easy to do."

She nodded, her face serious.

I nudged her. "Anyway, forget school. Let's think about the bakery. I didn't tell you, but you know that moody boy who comes into the bakery with his mum? The one who plays tennis?"

She nodded. "George? The one who never smiles?"

"That's right. Mum's been asked to make a tennis cake for him."

"Oooh." Mia looked excited. "What kind of tennis cake?"

"Well, that's not been decided yet. Mum and I had a few ideas . . ."

We talked about the cake all the way to the bakery. When we turned into the quiet street and I saw the Sugar and Spice sign swinging outside the front window I felt a swell of happiness.

39

The bell tinkled as we opened the door, and
I breathed in. Coffee, sugar, cinnamon, cake.
There wasn't a nicer combination of smells
in the world. Looking around the shop,
I saw that the wicker bread baskets were
almost empty – the bakery must have been
busy again. The middle shelf of the counter
was empty too, but the top shelf was filled
with sugary jam doughnuts, triple chocolate
cookies, cupcakes iced with pink-and-white
buttercream, and a tray of éclairs bursting
with cream. There were some fruit pies on

the bottom shelf and, in the warming cabinet, some fresh sausage rolls and cheese twists for people wanting a savoury snack on the way home.

Paula was polishing the counter top. She smiled when she saw us. "Hello, girls. How was school?"

"Good. We went to Baking Club," I said. "We made cookies."

"The teacher really liked them," said Mia, closing the door behind her. "She liked them so much she asked us to write an article for the school magazine."

"Ah!" Paula said. "I knew something good would happen today. It said so in your horoscopes. Here!" She pulled a magazine out from behind the counter and read. "Leo." She looked at me. "'Today is your chance to shine: seize every opportunity to show how capable you are!' And Pisces." That was Mia. "'People in positions of authority will be impressed, and hard work will reap great rewards.' See, it's there – written in the stars!"

Mia and I exchanged looks and tried not to giggle. Paula loved horoscopes, and no matter what happened in a day she would tell us that the stars had foretold it.

Just then, Mum came out from the kitchen at the back of the shop, dusting her hands on her apron. "Hi, girls. How was school?"

"Good. Do you want to try one of our cookies?" I said, taking the lid off my tin. We told her about Baking Club.

"These are delicious," Mum said. "And that's great about the article. What will you do it on?"

"Well, we want to do something that shows people how much fun baking is," I said.

"What about some interesting recipes for cupcakes and tips on how to make them?" suggested Paula.

I nodded.

Mum agreed. "Everyone likes cupcakes and you could give instructions for doing fun decorations."

"The cupcakes you sold at the belly-dancing fundraiser went down a storm," said Paula.

Mia and I had run a cake stall to help raise money for Paula's nephew, Tom.

"How is Tom?" Mia asked.

"No better," Paula said, with a sigh. "But the good news is that all the TV coverage of the belly dance helped us raise loads more money, so he'll be able to go to America in a few weeks."

"I hope it works," I said.

"Me too, sweetie," said Paula.

The doorbell tinkled and a customer came in with two small children. Mia and I went through to the tiny staffroom to drop our bags and wash our hands. There were some cake designs on Mum's desk. They were for the tennis cake.

"What do you think?" Mum said, following us.

"Wow. They're all good. I like this one best, I think," I said, picking up a sketch of a cake that looked like a tennis court with a boy on top holding a trophy.

The door tinkled again and Paula called, "Rose! Sarah King's here about the cake!"

"Let's see if our customer likes it too," said Mum. She gathered up her drawings and headed out to the shop.

5

George's mum, Sarah, was chatting to Paula
by the counter. She was small and neat-
looking, dressed in a salmon-pink skirt and
matching blouse – she was like a little pink
macaroon, perfectly made with no rough
edges. George was slumped on
the sofa in the corner, staring
at his feet. I had no idea what
kind of bake he would be –
there was no pastry or cake
that was spiky or bad-
tempered enough. Surely
today when he was here
to talk about a cake that was
being made especially for him,

he should be happy and excited? I would be!

Mia slipped away to help Paula. She's still shy around people she doesn't know, but I was keen to find out what they thought of Mum's sketches.

"These are great," Sarah said, leafing through. "Look, George. I like this one the best."

She held up my favourite design.

George glanced at it without interest.

"I can make the sugar model look just like George," Mum said.

"That would be fab," said Sarah. "What do you think, George?"

He shrugged. "Get whatever. I don't care."

My mouth fell open. I couldn't believe how rude he was being. I could see from Mum's expression that she was surprised too, but she hid it well. She always says we have to be polite to customers, no matter how they behave.

Sarah looked embarrassed. "George!" She turned to us. "I'm so sorry, he's tired. He was up before school playing tennis and he's got another coaching session this evening. He works really hard."

So hard he can't be nice? I thought.

"Do you play a lot of tennis, George?" Mum said.

He gave a brief nod.

"He plays in tournaments all over the country." Sarah's eyes glowed with pride. "His coach thinks he'll make junior Wimbledon in another few years."

George sank further into the sofa.

Oh, so that was it. He thought he was some kind of tennis god who didn't need to be nice to the rest of the world. I scowled at him.

"That's very impressive," Mum said. "So, what sort of cake would you like, George? Chocolate? Lemon? Carrot? Coffee?"

"Chocolate, please." He shot her a quick look. "And, um . . . thanks for making it."

Mum's face softened into a smile. "That's my pleasure." My glare lessened slightly too.

"When do you think it will be ready?" Sarah asked.

"Saturday afternoon. You can either call in or I could deliver it when we close – about 4 o'clock?"

"If you could deliver it that would be perfect. We have so much to do on Saturday! Thanks so much," said Sarah. She told Mum her address. "Come on then, George. Time for tennis."

"Can I get a sausage roll first?" he said.

"OK," Sarah said, handing him some money. There was now a queue of people at the counter. "I'll go and fetch the car. See you in a minute."

I hurried to help Paula. As I went behind the counter, I spotted Alice, who had just come in with her grandma, Mrs Rees, and waved.

Mia was serving the person in front of
Alice and Mrs Rees, a man called Dennis. He
was quite old and always gloomy. Everything
about him looked like it was sinking
downwards. There was nothing
bright and bouncy about
him at all. He reminded
me of a collapsed
sponge cake.

Dennis

"It's been a
lovely day, hasn't it, Mr
Henshaw?" Mia said, as
she put an apricot tart in a box for him.

He grunted. "It's been passable. Tomorrow
will be terrible, though," he said. "Rain and
wind all day, you mark my words. Hmph."
He shuffled along to pay Paula.

I caught Alice's eye and we both grinned.
"What would you like today, Mrs Rees?" I
asked.

Mrs Rees smiled vaguely. I realised her
hearing aid mustn't be working properly.
Alice raised her voice. "Gran! Hannah's
asking you what you would like."

"A chocolate éclair or maybe a custard slice?" I suggested.

"A custard slice for me today, please, dear," Mrs Rees said. "And whatever Alice wants."

Alice chose a doughnut.

I used the tongs to pick the cakes up and put them carefully into a box. "How's your dog? Is he better?" I asked Mrs Rees.

Mrs Rees blinked. "There's going to be fog? What? Tomorrow?"

Alice tried not to giggle.

"No, Mrs Rees. I said, how's your dog?" I tried to remember which of her dogs it was. "Bobby's been sick, hasn't he?"

"Yes, poor Bobby," said Mrs Rees. "He had to stay over at the vet's for the night, but he's back home now."

"That's good," I said. "You must be pleased. I could come round at the weekend and walk him for you, if you like?"

"No, I don't need a fork, dear," said Mrs Rees. "I've got plenty. Thank you!" I heard a muffled hiccup of laughter from beside her as she took the box and went to pay Paula, with Alice shaking her head in embarrassment. I looked up to see George chuckling.

He looked totally different without the scowl on his face.

"It's her hearing aid," I said frostily. "It doesn't work very well."

"Lucky you didn't ask her if she wanted a fruit tart, then," he whispered back.

I frowned, not quite understanding.

"Well, imagine if she'd misheard that."

I stifled a snort of laughter. He grinned. "Can I have a sausage roll, please?"

"Sure," I said. I put the sausage roll in a bag.

This was a surprise. Where had the bad-tempered, sulky George gone? So he *could* be nice after all.

"Thanks." He grinned as I handed it to him, and went to pay Paula.

I stared after him. As I turned around,

I saw Mia and Alice giggling together and looking at me.

"What?" I said, as George left.

"What were you and that boy whispering about?" Alice said.

"Nothing," I said.

"We think he likes you," said Mia.

Alice giggled again.

I shook my head. "You're both crazy. He doesn't like me and I definitely don't like him."

Mrs Rees turned to Alice. "Are you ready to go, Alice?"

Alice nodded. "See you tomorrow," she said to me and Mia.

"See you!" Mia and I called.

By five o'clock, the sign on the door was turned to closed, Paula had gone home and Mum was finishing up in the kitchen. Mia and I sat on the sofa, picking at a couple of leftover lemon cupcakes.

"I wish homework didn't exist," I said, as I thought about the pile of stuff I had to do that night.

"I know," Mia said, licking the buttercream icing off her fingers. "It should be banned. They should let us just relax when we're not in school."

"Or set us baking homework," I said.

"Definitely. I wouldn't mind doing that at all." Mia stretched. "I should go. Mum's taking me shopping."

"What for?"

"Oh, just some things for school," said Mia, flushing a little.

"OK, just quickly then, what do you think we should do the magazine article on?" I said.

Mia paused for a moment. "Maybe cupcakes, like Paula and your mum suggested?"

"I've been thinking about that. There are bound to have been articles on cupcakes already," I said. "Even people who hardly do any baking at all will have made cupcakes. Maybe we should do something more unusual. Like Danish pastries."

"But making Danishes is going to be way too much work for most people," Mia argued. "They'd probably think 'why bother?' and stop reading."

She had a point.

"So, what can we write about that's easy and also interesting?" I wondered.

Mia's eyes fell on the stands where Mum displayed the wedding and birthday cakes she'd made. "What about cakes?" she said. "Not cupcakes, but special occasion cakes."

"Yes, and what about a section on icing them too?" I said, getting excited.

"And making fondant figures!" said Mia.

"And how to display them," I said.

"We can take loads of pictures here," said Mia. "We could even interview your mum. I bet no one's ever interviewed a proper baker before."

"It's a brilliant idea," I said. "You're a genius!" I beamed at her.

"We'll have to do some baking ourselves," said Mia. "And put in a few different recipes."

"And do some cake decorating too," I said happily. If only we didn't have boring homework to do. I couldn't wait to get started!

NOTES ON THE ARTICLE

- Things to include: different types of cake - fruit? sponge?
- Different types of sponges. Recipe for a lemon sponge, a chocolate sponge, a carrot cake? Arrow to this and words: we need to do lots of experimenting!
- Different types of icing - royal icing, buttercream icing, fondant icing.
- Interview with Mum.

LOTS OF PHOTOS OF THE CAKES IN THE BAKERY!

Lemon cupcakes

Eclairs

6

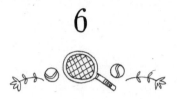

Next morning, for once I was awake earlier than Molly and Ella. My journal had fallen to the floor beside my bed. I'd been making notes for the Baking Club article before I fell asleep.

I picked it up and added some more ideas – Mum always had display cakes in the shop. We could take pictures of those, and I knew she had a new wedding cake to make, as well as George's tennis cake. We could take photos of those when they were finished. I kept my fingers crossed that our article would also help spread the word about Mum and her brilliant cakes. I know how much she loves creating them – and I love helping her.

When Mia called for me on the way to school, I noticed something was different about her. I couldn't work out what it was at first, then as we walked down the road I realised. "You've got new shoes!"

They were just like mine.

Mia looked a bit embarrassed. "Yeah. I hope you don't mind. I thought my old ones were a bit babyish. No one else wears shoes with straps across the foot." It was true – nearly everyone else at school has ballet pumps or black leather trainers.

"They look good," I said, meaning it. "And I don't mind at all. Half the school wears them."

She smiled. "Thanks."

As we walked on, I noticed Mia hadn't tied her hair back as she usually did. After our conversation yesterday she must have decided to change how she looked. I was pleased. Maybe now she would feel that she fitted in more.

"OMG, Mia! You've got new shoes!" Misha exclaimed, as Mia and I arrived at the lockers.

"And you've left your hair down," said Alice. "I like it."

Mia blushed, pleased, but embarrassed to have everyone looking at her. "Thanks."

"All you need now is a different bag and a shorter skirt and you'll look completely normal!" Misha said half-teasingly. "Why don't you turn your skirt over at the waistband? That'll make it shorter."

Mia looked at her skirt. "What do you mean?"

"Here." Misha showed her how to turn her skirt over at the top to make it shorter. "See," she said. "That's much better."

"Oh." Mia looked down at her skirt and smiled. "Thanks, Misha."

It was a bit weird watching Mia worrying about things like her skirt length. OK, I was the one who had told her that she should change the way she looked if she wanted to, but seeing it happen felt wrong somehow.

"Anyway," Misha said, twirling round and

getting our attention. "My turn now. What do you all think of my new bag?"

She posed, turning this way and that showing off her bag. It was a leather handbag with lots of pockets and buckles, like some of the Year 7 and 8 girls had. We oohed and ahhed enviously.

"I love it," I said. Then, only half-joking, "Can I have it?"

"No," Misha said, holding her bag protectively. "It's all mine!"

"You're so lucky," said Lara. "I'd love a handbag like that. Mum says they're not practical, though."

"Who cares about practical?" Misha said. "Mums have no idea!" She got a lip gloss out of her bag. "Anyone want some? It's watermelon and pomegranate flavour."

We passed it round. I thought Mia wouldn't be interested because I've never seen her wearing any make-up, not even lip gloss, but Misha nudged her. "Go on, why don't you try it? It'll look nice."

Mia hesitated and then dabbed a bit on her finger. "OK." She rubbed it onto her lips.

"It suits you," Misha said.

Mia smiled. It was a relief to see her looking relaxed with the others for once. Her happy mood continued for the rest of the day. At lunchtime, Misha, Lara and Alice started talking about the new Ellie B album again. To my surprise, Mia had actually persuaded her mum to buy it for her the night before and, not only that, she'd also listened to it.

"'Red Arrow' is definitely the best song," Lara said.

"Yeah, I love the chorus," Mia agreed.

"We should all save up and go to an Ellie B concert," Alice said.

"Yeah, definitely!" said Mia.

I started to feel a bit strange as I listened to them talk. Usually when Misha, Alice and Lara start talking about music or other stuff they're into that Mia and I aren't – like ponies – Mia and I just chat together. It was weird that she was able to join in with them and I wasn't. I wondered if I should ask to borrow the album from Mia tonight, but decided that was silly. I'm not into Ellie B and I didn't want to spend the evening listening to it just so I could join in when they talked about it.

I looked up and saw Mia trying to flick her hair over her shoulders like Alice always did. I hadn't seen her do that before.

"Are you OK?" Alice said, glancing at me.

I realised I was frowning. "Yeah, I'm fine," I said. "Just thinking about something."

"Cakes, no doubt!" Alice grinned.

"Yep!" I lied. I pushed away thoughts of Mia. She was just trying to fit in. There wasn't anything wrong with that, was there?

When the bakery shut that day, I stayed on to help Mum decorate George's tennis cake. Mum had baked it in the afternoon. It was very chocolatey and had three layers of sponge sandwiched together with a rich chocolate buttercream. Mum was going to top it with a chocolate ganache, then add a tennis court made from pale green fondant icing to the top. She'd make an icing sugar net, a tennis racquet and a sugar model of George with a trophy in his hands. First, we coated the entire cake with a layer of buttercream, then we made the ganache. Mum added butter to dark chocolate and placed the bowl over a pan of boiling water. I stirred with a spoon, watching the butter and chocolate melt and swirl together. The smell was heavenly.

MY SHORT CUT CHOCOLATE GANACHE RECIPE

Perfect for topping a chocolate cake when you want a really glossy shiny finish.

You will need:

A chocolate cake (for topping)
360g dark chocolate
250g unsalted butter
2 tablespoons golden syrup

What to do:

1. Break the chocolate into squares and chop the butter into cubes.

2. Melt all the ingredients together in a heavy-based saucepan over a very low heat, stirring all the time, until the mixture is smooth and glossy with no lumps.

3. Place your cake on a wire rack with lots of greaseproof paper underneath to catch the spills.

4. Ladle the ganache over the cake, using a palette knife to cover any gaps. Work quickly before the mixture starts to set.

5. Top the cake with any decorations – my favourites are sugar flowers or whipped cream or fresh fruit.

Top Tip:

Don't touch the icing once it has started to harden or the shiny finish will be spoilt!

Mum started to roll out the different colours of icing paste to make the figure. When other bakers put figures on cakes, they often look clumsy and lumpy, but not Mum's. She's brilliant at sculpting sugar paste. I knew she would make the figure look just like George.

"Now bring the cream to boil in another saucepan," Mum told me.

I did as she said, trying to keep stirring the chocolate and butter mixture at the same time. Sometimes you feel like you need two sets of hands when you're baking!

"So, how's everything going at school?" Mum asked.

"Good," I said. "The teachers are mostly OK and the work's not bad."

"How about your friends?" Mum said. "How are you all getting on?"

"Um . . . fine."

"But?" Mum said, looking at me.

Mum always knows if there's something I'm not telling her and, in the warmth of the bakery kitchen, with just the two of us, it felt easy to talk. "No, everyone's good. It's just Mia."

"What about her?" Mum asked.

"She's worried the others don't like her and she's started changing how she looks – and getting into new music."

"Trying to fit in is quite normal at your age," Mum said. "People want to be like their friends. You asked Alice what kind of shoes and bag everyone at King William's had before you started, so you could buy the right stuff and fit in – why shouldn't Mia?"

I frowned. Mum was right. I *had* done that. It just felt a bit odd seeing Mia do it now. I tried to explain. "I know. I guess the thing is that Mia never normally bothers about how she looks and she's never talked about music. It's like she's keeping her true self a secret and trying to be the Mia she thinks people want her to be."

"Ah." Mum nodded slowly. "Well, that's different. It's one thing trying to fit in, but pretending to be something you're not isn't a recipe for happiness. I hope Mia realises that."

"Should I say something?" I said.

Mum gave me a sympathetic look. "You can't really, love. Mia has to figure it out for herself. All you can do is be there for her and be a good friend."

That's one of the cool things about Mum. She listens whenever I have problems and she doesn't tell me that things can all be sorted out easily. She gets that sometimes it's hard and there isn't a magic solution. I felt better just having talked to her about it. "Thanks, Mum. I love you," I said.

She smiled. "I love you too. Now, how's that ganache coming on?"

I showed her the glossy smooth chocolate mixture in the pan.

"Perfect!" she said. "Leave that to cool for a few minutes, and come and make a mini tennis racquet out of icing."

When the ganache was ready, Mum put greaseproof paper underneath the cake on its wire rack and I ladled the mixture carefully over the top, making sure we covered every bit of it. Then, together, we lifted the cake onto a cake stand and left it to set. It was time to start on the decorating!

By the time we had finished, it was dark outside – and the cake looked amazing. It had a lime-green tennis court of fondant icing on top, with piped white lines to mark the court. Mum had made a delicate net from royal icing. The fondant George figure was chilling in the fridge, along with the tennis racquet and two tennis balls I had made. The racquet had been fiddly but it looked great, even if I did say so myself!

"All done," Mum said. "We'll put it together tomorrow and take it over to their house after we shut the bakery. I hope they like it."

"How could they not?" I said. "It's brilliant!"

I stretched, my shoulders stiff from hunching over the bench. "I'm tired."

"Me too," Mum said, stifling a yawn.

"Thanks for staying with me. I'd have been here even longer without your help, love."

"Hmm." I pretended to consider it. "So, let's see . . . I could have had an evening of playing princesses and reading endless bedtime stories. Or I could have been here with you." I shook my head. "It was a hard choice, Mum."

Mum grinned. "The twins aren't that bad."

"I know," I admitted. "I'd just rather be baking with you."

"And I'd rather have you here with me," said Mum. She gave me a hug. "I'm very glad I opened the bakery."

I hugged her back. "I'm VERY glad you did too!" I said.

7

When Molly and Ella came flying into my
bedroom at half past six next morning, rather
than groaning and turning over like I had
been doing all week, I threw back my duvet
and jumped out of bed. It was Saturday.
Yay! That meant I could spend all day in
the bakery. Mia was meeting me there, there
would be lots of customers to talk to, and it
was Mum's new apprentice Dylan's first day.
I wondered what he would be like.

And FUN was the answer! Dylan was
tall and skinny and good-looking, with
spiky blond hair and green eyes. He was
really cheerful and he worked really hard.
Whenever I went into the kitchen he was

DYLAN

lifting or carrying things, moving trays of pastries or emptying flour into the dough brake.

He didn't seem to mind when Mum spoke to him sharply about putting the baking tins in the wrong place for the second time, or about moving her dough scraper from where she had left it.

"Sorry," he said. "I won't do it again, Rosie."

I glanced at Mum. Her name was Rose, and no one *ever* called her Rosie. But she didn't seem to mind. I soon discovered that Dylan was the sort of person who gives everyone nicknames.

"Hey, Skippy, how's it going?" he said, when I came to ask if there was anything ready to go out on the shelves.

"Skippy?"

He grinned. "Yeah, that's what I'm going to call you."

"Um . . . why?"

"You remind me of a kangaroo in an old kids' programme I used to watch. It was called Skippy – it was always bouncing around and being helpful. It was really cute."

Cute! A good-looking eighteen-year-old thought I was cute! I couldn't help blushing.

"Come on then, Skips, here are the loaves." He placed a wicker basket full of warm bread into my arms. "What now, Rosie?" he said, turning to Mum.

"The shortcrust pastry needs rolling out for the fruit pies," she said. "Can you get it out of the fridge?"

"No problem." He winked at me. "Laters, Skippy. There's work to do here."

Mia was nervous around him at first, but Dylan was the sort of person you couldn't be shy with for long. He called her Minnie because he said she reminded him of a mouse, and Minnie Mouse was his favourite mouse. She seemed to like having a nickname, or maybe it was just the way he smiled at her as he said it, with his very twinkly eyes.

Having Dylan around gave the bakery a new level of energy. Even when he had a break, he kept moving. He came out into the shop and straightened baskets, chatting to Paula, Mia and me as he drank his strong black coffee.

He calls Paula "Little Auntie Paula". He's known her all his life because she's a friend of his mum's, and he keeps trying to annoy her by patting the top of her head as if she was a child. She huffs and puffs at him every time he does it, but I can tell she doesn't mind really.

The morning flew by. We had a steady stream of customers and the bread baskets and counter were emptying fast. Dylan and Mum had to make extra bread, sausage rolls and cheese twists.

"Have you thought about doing meat pies?" Dylan asked Mum. "I bet they'd sell out. I make them all the time at home."

"What sort of recipes?"

"Steak and wild mushroom, pork and apple, game pie."

"They sound great," said Mum, nodding. "You'll have to show me."

I could see that Mum and Dylan were going to work really well together. I felt a twinge of jealousy. I would have loved to be in the kitchen with her, but I knew she needed someone who could be there every day. Bakeries need strict routines – that's what Mum always says. And, anyway, if I was in the kitchen I wouldn't be able to help in the shop and chat to the customers, and I do love doing that. At least I get to help in the kitchen when she's doing special cakes. George's finished cake was in the kitchen, waiting to be delivered. I couldn't wait to see what he and his mum thought of it!

Later that afternoon, Mum and I left Paula and Dylan to shut up the bakery, and set off to take the tennis cake to George and Sarah's house. They live about half a mile out of town. It's an old stone house, with old-fashioned windows, and it's seriously big, with a crescent-shaped driveway with posh gates.

As we drove through the gates, the front door opened and Sarah appeared. Mum took the lid off the cake box to show her the cake on the back seat of the car. Sarah caught her breath. "Oh my goodness, it's incredible! It's absolutely wonderful."

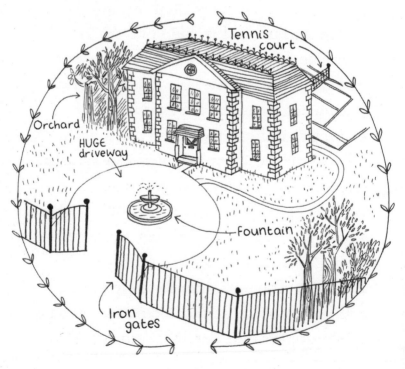

Tennis court

Orchard

HUGE driveway

Fountain

Iron gates

I had to agree. The model of George was now in place, the tennis racquet on the ground at his feet and the trophy, decorated with edible gold leaf, in his hands.

Mum picked up the box and carried it carefully inside. Sarah led the way to a huge stone-flagged kitchen. It was as big as the whole ground floor of our house! The table was covered with plates and plates of food, and there was a serving trolley filled with glasses and wine coolers.

Sarah made a space for the cake on the table, and Mum put it down.

Sarah went into the hall and called upstairs. "George! Come down. Your cake's here. Come and see!"

George came downstairs. I wondered what sort of mood he would be in. Would he be the fun George I'd got a glimpse of the other day, or would he be back to his usual grumpy self? He slouched into the kitchen with his hands in his pockets. Oh. Grumpy, then.

"What do you think?" Sarah said.

George gave the cake a quick look. "Yeah,

it's great." He turned to my mum. "Thanks."

That was all he was going to say? If I'd been given a cake like that I'd have been jumping up and down in delight. Frustration boiled up in me. Had he any idea how much work it had been?

"Would you like a coffee?" Sarah asked Mum.

"It's OK. We won't stay," Mum said. "You must have lots to do for tonight."

"Not at all," said Sarah. "I'm all sorted. I'd love to have a coffee if you have time."

"All right," Mum said, smiling. "Then that would be lovely."

"George, why don't you show Hannah around?" Sarah suggested.

My heart sank. I hoped he'd say no, but to my surprise he shrugged. "Sure." He turned to me. "Shall we get a drink? We can take them with us."

"OK." I really didn't want to have to spend time with him but I knew I had to be polite – even if politeness was something *he* apparently didn't understand.

We took two cans of Coke from the fridge and I followed him through to the rest of the house. We passed a cosy snug and a grand dining room with tennis pictures up on the walls, and went into a massive lounge with French windows, squashy sofas and a cabinet full of trophies.

I went over to the cabinet and looked at his trophies. "So . . . how long have you been playing tennis?"

"Since I was three," he said, folding his arms. He looked unimpressed, and I tried to think of something else to say.

"You've won lots of things," I said.

"Yeah."

"It must be amazing to go to all the different competitions."

"I guess," he said briefly.

An awkward silence fell. My heart sank even further. How long was Mum going to be with coffee? It would feel like forever if the conversation carried on like this.

"Should we go outside?" George said suddenly.

I nodded and he opened the French windows that led out onto a vast lawn with beds of roses and lavender.

He took a deep breath of fresh air, as if the lounge had been stifling him.

"So what do you do when you're not playing tennis?" I asked.

"I used to play rugby and I was learning to play the drums last year. But I don't have time any more. Now I'm up at five every morning to play tennis before school. I go to school, do homework, play more tennis. That's it. That's my life." He gave a short bitter laugh.

I felt a prickle of irritation. "It can't be that bad. After all, you do *like* playing tennis, don't you?"

"'Course I do," he said quickly. Then he changed the subject. "What about you? What do you like doing when you're not baking or at school?"

I shrugged. "Just hanging out with my friends, really. The usual."

"Do you go to King William's?"

I nodded.

"Is it strange going to a school with boys and girls together?"

"No, it's normal," I said in surprise. "Is it strange for you going to a school with just boys?"

"No, it's normal," he echoed. We half-smiled at each other and the awkwardness seemed to melt a little bit.

We started talking about our schools. They sounded pretty similar, although his teachers were called "masters" and he did Latin as one of his subjects. He told me about some tricks he and his friends had played and did imitations of the masters, and I told him all about my friends and the bakery and some of the funny things the customers did. I realised we had a similar sense of humour and that we were good at making each other laugh. I was surprised at how easy he was to talk to.

We went into the orchard and he showed me how he could hang upside-down from one of the apple trees. I did it too – mainly because he seemed to think I wouldn't because I was a girl.

"Told you!" I said, dangling upside-down from the branch and looking at him. Then I swung myself back upwards until I was sitting on the branch.

"You're pretty cool for a girl," he said.

There weren't any apples on the trees, it was too early in the year, but I picked a handful of leaves and threw them at him. "Oi! What do you mean, for a *girl*?"

He grinned. "Well, everyone knows girls aren't as good as boys."

I could tell he was just saying it to wind me up but I pretended to be outraged. "Take that back!" I scrambled down and lunged at him.

He dodged away.

I chased him all around the orchard and lawn without catching him. At last we stopped. I was puffing and red-cheeked but he was barely out of breath. He must be super-fit from all the tennis.

"OK, I give up," I said, sitting down on the grass.

He sat down beside me. "Told you girls were rubbish."

"Ha ha." I was too hot to argue. I flopped back instead and looked at the blue sky and white clouds. George lay back as well. "This is fun," he said. "I almost never get to just hang out. I'm always too busy practising."

"I guess you have to practise a lot if you want to win," I said.

"Yeah." He gave that short hard laugh again. "And that's all that matters."

I glanced at him. For someone whose life revolved around tennis, he didn't sound as if he enjoyed it much.

I rolled onto my tummy and looked at him. Suddenly, the smiling, laughing George had gone.

"George! Hannah!" We sat up. George's mum was calling us from the French windows. "It's time for Hannah to go and, George, you need to get ready for the party."

We got to our feet. George's shoulders slumped and as we walked back I saw the bad mood descend on him again. Why? We'd been having so much fun messing around in the orchard.

We went into the kitchen. Mum was waiting to go. "Have you had fun?" she asked.

"Yeah." And I really had.

"You must come again," Sarah said to Mum. "I've really enjoyed it. It's nice to talk to someone who isn't anything to do with tennis."

"Well, it's nice for me having a chance to chat to someone about things other than the bakery," said Mum. "I don't think I've sat down to have a coffee with anyone this past couple of weeks. The bakery can feel a bit all-consuming at times."

"Like George's tennis!" Sarah said with a smile. "It takes up every moment. I'm always running around after him."

"Poor Hannah doesn't get me running around after her at all," said Mum. "I'm too busy with the bakery."

"It must be amazing – having your own business," Sarah said to Mum. "I dreamed of doing that once."

"What? Having a bakery?" Mum asked.

"No." Sarah laughed. "I'm useless at baking. I wanted to start my own business selling herbal beauty lotions and potions. When I was younger my mother had a hairdressing salon. I did a bit of hairdressing with her, but what I really loved was making herbal conditioners and shampoos. Later I started making bath oils and bath bombs and body butters too. I went on a course. I planned to have a little shop near the town centre."

"Why didn't you?" Mum asked.

"Oh, it was around the time George was talent-spotted and started having lots of coaching. I wanted to support him and I couldn't open a business at the same time."

George shuffled uncomfortably.

"That's a shame," Mum said.

Sarah smiled. "Oh, I don't mind. It's been worth it, hasn't it, George?"

He shrugged. "Yeah. I guess."

Sarah laughed. "And that's all the thanks I get. Teenagers!"

I frowned. Something was seriously up with George. Whenever tennis was mentioned he just clammed up and got in a bad mood. Why?

Mum took her car keys out of her pocket. "Right, we'd better go. I hope the party goes well tonight."

"Thanks. Shall we drop the cake stand back to the shop on Monday?" Sarah asked. "Or I could drop it in at your house tomorrow?"

"Whichever suits," Mum said. "You're more than welcome to pop round to the bakery for a coffee tomorrow – I'm showing Hannah how to make Danish pastries and working on a wedding cake."

"Great," said Sarah. "We'll call in on our

way home from George's morning practice then – about twelve?"

"Perfect," said Mum.

"Before we go, would you mind if I took a photo of the cake?" I asked. "I'm writing an article about baking for our school magazine and I'd love to put a picture of this cake in."

"OK," Sarah said.

I got out my phone and took a few photos.

"George, you should be in the photo," Mum said.

"Yes," said Sarah. "Go on."

He looked a bit embarrassed, but he stood by the cake and I got the photo I wanted.

We said our goodbyes and got into the car.

"What a nice family," said Mum as we drove away. "Sarah's lovely. George seems a bit shy, though."

"Shy?" I said. "He's not shy. He talked loads when we were outside."

"Maybe he's just shy with adults then," Mum said. "But you got on OK with him?"

"Yeah. We got on really well in the end. Though he didn't seem to want to talk about tennis. It's strange; I thought he wouldn't want to talk about anything else."

"Maybe he's embarrassed. Sarah says he wins a lot."

I frowned. I hadn't got the impression George was embarrassed. "I don't think he likes tennis very much," I said.

"Don't be silly!" Mum laughed. "His whole life is tennis. He must like it."

I didn't say anything. I knew it sounded odd, but it was just a feeling I had.

"I hope they do call in for a coffee tomorrow," Mum went on.

I nodded. I hoped so too. I wanted to see George again and get to know him better. I really liked him, but at the moment I just couldn't work him out at all.

8

Mum and I headed to the bakery after breakfast on Sunday morning. I felt light and happy as we walked down the road. A morning of baking with Mum – what could be better?

We started with the Danish pastry dough that we'd made yesterday evening. Mum showed me how to roll it out and coat it with a block of softened butter, before folding it like a letter and then rolling it again. This was called 'laminating' the dough. Then she wrapped the dough in cling film and put it in the fridge for an hour. She said that we would have to take it out twice more to roll it and fold it again. It's all the folding that gives the pastries their flaky, buttery layers. Yum!

In between preparing the dough, we started on the different tiers of the wedding cake Mum was baking for a customer. People usually wanted fruit cake for a wedding, but this bride wanted four different flavours of sponge.

When at last the cakes were cooling and the Danish pastry dough was chilling for the final time in the fridge, there was a knock on the front door. It was Sarah and George.

"That's good timing," Mum said, letting them in. "We were just about to take a break. Would you like a coffee?"

"I'd love one," Sarah said. I noticed she looked a bit stressed. I glanced at George and saw that he was scowling. He stood with his arms folded, ignoring me. I tried to catch his eye, but he was too busy glaring at his mum. I guessed they must have just had a row.

"What would you like, Sarah?" Mum said, going to the coffee machine. "Cappuccino? Latte? Espresso?"

"A cappuccino would be lovely," said

Sarah, sitting on the sofa.

"George? Would you like a drink?" Mum asked.

He shook his head. "No, thank you." He spoke politely but when Mum turned away, he resumed glaring at the back of Sarah's head.

"Do you want to come through to the kitchen?" I asked him, hoping to distract him.

He nodded and followed me through into the kitchen.

As soon as the door shut behind him, he pushed his hands through his hair. "I can't believe her!" he burst out.

"Your mum?"

"Yeah." He stomped around the bakery. "I spent all yesterday evening at this stupid party she'd organised with all her friends from the tennis club, and yet today when I asked her on the way here if I can have tonight off to play the drums with Alec and Callum, she said no, because guess what? I have to practise my tennis!" He thumped a fist on the pastry bench. "One night off, that's all I wanted. I never ask for time off. Never. But oh no. It's fine when it's for a party she wants to throw to boast about how great her son is, but not when I just want to go and chill and have fun."

I didn't know what to say. "That . . . that does seem a bit harsh."

"Harsh? All I do is practise, practise, practise. I haven't had a night out with my friends in months."

He glowered at me for a moment and then shook his head "Look, sorry. I'm not angry with you. It's my mum. I just wish . . . well, I wish I didn't have to play tennis all the time."

His words hung in the air. I didn't know what to say. He took a breath and looked round as if he was seeing the kitchen properly for the first time. "I've never been in a bakery kitchen before. What do all these things do?" he asked, going over to the big dough brake and then peering inside the flour bins.

I showed George around, explaining everything. It wasn't a big kitchen, but by the time I'd shown him everything, his bad mood seemed to have faded. He took two knives out of the knife block.

"What did one knife say to another?"

"What?" I said.

He grinned. "Look sharp!"

I giggled. "OK, what did one slice of bread say to another when he saw the butter and jam on the table?"

"What?"

"We're toast!"

"That's terrible!" he said.

"You can talk! Do you want a drink?" I said, opening the fridge.

He peered over my shoulder. "Yes, please – have you got any Coke?"

I passed him one and he pulled back the tab. For a moment we drank in a companionable silence. I thought about what he had said earlier.

"Do you really practise *all* the time?" I asked.

He sighed. "Yep. When I'm not at school or doing my homework, anyway."

I tried to imagine it. It would be like me having to bake all the time . . . but, actually, I couldn't see anything wrong with that. "Isn't that OK, though?" I went on cautiously. "I mean, you love tennis, don't you?"

He didn't reply.

"You must do," I said.

"Of course I love it . . ." He broke off. "You know, I'm sick of lying. No, actually, I don't love it. I used to, but these last few years it's all become so intense. All the coaching, all the practice, all the tournaments. I hate that side of it."

"Seriously?"

He nodded. "I just want to hang out with friends, play my drums, go on the computer – do normal stuff." He flushed as his eyes met mine and I had the feeling he was regretting having said anything. "Look, I haven't told anyone this before. It's a secret, OK?"

I frowned. "You haven't told your mum?"

He shook his head. "I can't. She's put so

much into me becoming a big tennis star. It's been her life since I was little. I can't tell her I don't want to do it any more. She'll be gutted."

"But you can't keep playing if you hate it," I said.

He shrugged. "I have to."

"Which is why you're always so moody when you're on your way to tennis coaching and why you never want to talk about tennis," I realised. "I thought you were really horrible when I first met you."

He had the grace to look ashamed. "Sorry."

"You really should talk to your mum," I said. I knew he was right and she'd probably be really upset, but I was also sure she'd want to know.

"I can't," he said again. "And you can't tell her or your mum or anyone else either. OK?"

"OK," I said reluctantly. "I promise."

Just then our mums came in. "What are you up to in here?" Mum asked.

"Just talking," I said quickly.

"Great – well, the Danish dough should be

about ready," said Mum.

"We should get going," said Sarah. "Sunday afternoon is George's homework time and then he has tennis practice."

George rolled his eyes at me.

"Look, here's my number," I said, scribbling my mobile number on a piece of paper. "Phone or text me."

"Thanks." He took the paper.

"Maybe we can meet up some time," I said.

He nodded, but I could tell he was thinking that he would probably be too busy. He and his mum left.

"Time to get the dough out," said Mum.

I tried to stop thinking about George, but it was hard. I felt so sorry for him. I could understood why he didn't want to say anything. It would be like me telling my mum I didn't want to bake any more. But I know Mum would want to know if something was making me unhappy, and I was sure Sarah would too.

Mum explained how to cut and fold the pastry to make different shapes. We made chocolate chip snails, raspberry pinwheels and strawberry envelopes. Then they rested for a while before going in the oven. When they came out they were crisp and buttery, golden brown on top, and filled with melting jam or dotted with chocolate chips. They looked delicious!

We took the pastries home to share with Mark and the twins. We sat down round the kitchen table. First, though, I took some photos of them and sent them to Mia. "Soooo jealous!" she texted back. "Promise you'll teach me how to make them!"

"I will! C u 2mrw!"

Then I saw the look Mum was giving me – it was the *get-off-your-phone-now-if-you-know-what's-good-for-you-young-lady* look. I put my phone away and sat down. The pastries were delicious – light, buttery, crispy layers with a soft and sweet middle. My favourites were the chocolate chip snails.

"Can you make these again?" asked Molly.

"Every Sunday, please," said Mark, munching on a raspberry pinwheel. "These are amazingly good."

"Superdog says they're super WOOF!" said Ella.

Looking round the now very crumby and jammy kitchen table and listening to my family laugh and chat, I thought of George doing his homework so that he could get to bed early and then get up at five o'clock to play tennis – which he didn't even really want to do. Despite his big house and his luxury lifestyle, I knew I would far rather be me.

When you have shaped them, they need to sit for a little while before going in the oven. If you bake them too soon, they will be cakey and solid, but if you leave them too long they will have a breadcrumby texture. Mum says there's a point where they are at their best to go in, but you can only really learn when that is by making lots of them. (That's fine by me!)

Choc chip snails

Strawberry envelopes

Raspberry pinwheels

9

Alice texted me in the morning:

> Do u want 2 come 2 Harry's after schl? Mum's given me money so I can take everyone 4 an early bday treat.

I was surprised. I hadn't known it was her birthday. That was typical of Alice. If it had been Misha's birthday, she'd have talked about nothing else! Harry's was the local ice-cream parlour and I was always up for a trip there, so I replied straight away.

> *Yes pls! When's ur bday?*

> Sun, but not having a party. It's my cousin's bday 2 and we're doing a family trip at the wkend. C u soon. X

When Mia arrived to walk to school I saw that she had a new bag – a canvas one covered with pictures of cupcakes. Her hair was down again and she was wearing lip gloss.

"Do you like my bag?" she asked.

"Yeah, it's great. I love it!" I said. I really did.

"Do you want some lip gloss?" she said, offering me a little round pot.

"Thanks," I said. The lip gloss was the same watermelon and pomegranate one that Misha had. I was a bit surprised. I knew I wouldn't have chosen exactly the same flavour as one of my friends had, in case they thought I was copying them. I mean, wearing the same shoes is one thing, but you want to be a bit different with stuff like lip glosses and hair slides and bags.

When we got to school, Mia showed the others her new bag.

Misha rolled her eyes. "Cupcakes – what a surprise. Don't you ever think of anything except baking?"

I knew she was only teasing but Mia looked disappointed.

"I think Mia's bag is great," I said.

Misha stroked her own bag. "Sorry. This is really the *only* type of bag to have."

Alice shook her head at her in exasperation. "I like your bag too, Mia," she said.

Mia gave a small smile.

"So," Alice changed the subject. "Who's looking forward to Harry's this afternoon?"

We all were. We started talking about the ice creams we would have. Harry's does the best ice-cream sundaes and banana splits in the world!

I was very happy when the day was over and we made our way to the ice-cream parlour. It was fun walking into town together. "What are you getting for your birthday?" I asked Alice.

"Mum's finally said I can have my hair dip-dyed!" Alice said. "I'm going to the hairdresser's tomorrow."

"Awesome! My mum said I can have mine done in the summer holidays," said Misha. "But I've had to promise I'll cut the ends off before school starts again."

"I want to have mine done too," Mia said.

I looked at her in surprise. She hadn't mentioned it to me before. I didn't want to be mean but I thought her hair was probably a bit short for dip-dyeing and, being strawberry blonde, it wasn't quite the right colour. It would just look odd.

"We should have a dip-dyeing party and dye our hair together," said Misha. "You can buy kits to do it at home."

"Really?" said Mia.

"Yeah," said Misha. "We could have a sleepover and do it then."

I could just imagine my mum's reaction to that. "And be grounded for life? No, thank you!" I said, laughing.

Harry's was quiet and we managed to get one of the best tables – a semi-circular red leather booth. As the others squeezed in, I saw George and his mum sitting at a table opposite. He was drinking a hot chocolate and flicking through a magazine and she was reading a book.

I went over. "Hi," I said.

George looked around and smiled. "Oh, hi, Hannah."

"Hello," Sarah said. "Are you here with your mum?"

"No, just some school friends," I said, nodding towards our booth. "Do you want to join us?" I said to George.

He looked at his mum.

"That's fine if you want to," she said. "I've got my book."

"OK," he said, picking up his hot chocolate. "Thanks."

We walked back over.

"This is George, everyone," I said. "He's one of our regulars at the bakery and Mum's just made a cake for him."

Misha grinned at him. "Hi, George. I'm Misha." Everyone introduced themselves then we decided on our ice creams.

"What are you going to have, Mia?" I asked.

"I don't know. Maybe a strawberry sundae. What about you?" she said.

"I haven't decided yet," I said.

"I'm going to have a chocolate and toffee sundae," said Misha.

"Oh, I'll have that too then," said Mia.

I sighed. I wished that she would choose something *she* liked and not just copy other people.

In the end I chose a banana split. While we waited for our ice creams, Misha quizzed George about his school. He asked about our school too, and what clubs we did.

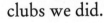

"Lara and I do netball," said Misha. "But most of the other clubs are just lame, like computer club, sewing club or . . ." She shot a look towards me and Mia, "Baking Club. I mean, who'd go to a club like that?"

"Ha ha!" I said, pulling a face at her. "Mia and I go to Baking Club," I explained to George. "And it's not lame at all."

"She's really excited because she's been asked to write some geeky article for the school mag," said Misha. "It's totally tragic."

"Mia and I don't think it's tragic, do we, Mia?" I said, turning to her. "We like Baking Club."

Mia glanced from Misha to me. Misha raised her eyebrows at her.

"Um . . . well . . . I guess it's not the coolest thing ever," Mia said. "It is a bit boring."

Misha gave a delighted hoot. "See, Baking Club *is* lame! It is! Even Mia thinks so!"

I stared at Mia. I couldn't believe what she'd just said. She avoided my gaze. I think Alice must have realised how shocked I was, because she changed the subject.

"So, how long have you been playing tennis, George?" Alice asked. "And have you ever met anyone famous?"

George told us about having met Andy Murray and Tim Henman. I was half-listening but I kept thinking about how Mia had just agreed with Misha about Baking Club being lame. I *knew* she didn't really think that. She was just siding with Misha because she wanted to look good. I felt really cross with her; so cross I found it hard to enjoy the rest of the time at Harry's. George seemed to enjoy himself, though. He threw rolled-up paper napkins like Alice and Lara when Misha tried to sing along with the jukebox, and he had a competition with Misha to see who could fit the most ice-cream wafers into their mouth. He won that one.

When his mum finally came over, he looked really disappointed.

"Time for training," Sarah said.

George heaved a sigh. "See you guys. It's been fun."

"Bye," we chorused.

I watched him walk away with his mum. All the happiness seemed to have drained out of him now he was off to tennis.

"He's cute," Misha said as the door closed behind him.

Alice giggled. "I think he likes Hannah."

Misha nudged me. "Do you like him, Hannah?"

"Yes, but just as a friend," I said.

Misha's eyes glinted. "Hannah and George, up a tree . . ." she sang.

"Shut up!" I said, pushing her.

She giggled and pushed me back.

Alice's mum picked up Alice, Misha and Lara. She offered to give Mia and me a lift home, but we said we would walk back to the bakery and her mum's shop.

We set off down the street. Now we were alone I kept thinking about what she had said at Harry's. "Mia, why did you say that Baking Club is boring?" I asked.

She went red.

"Do you really think that?"

"No," she said.

"So why did you say it?"

She didn't answer.

I stared at her in frustration. "You said it just to look good in front of Misha, didn't you? Like saying earlier how you want to have your hair dip-dyed—"

"I do want to," she interrupted.

"You don't! I know you don't. And I know you're not really into Ellie B either, even though you keep talking about her. You're copying people all the time!"

"I'm not!"

"You are! You're just pretending to be someone you're not, so they'll like you. That's stupid."

Mia glared at me. "You're just jealous," she said. "You don't like it because suddenly I'm getting on with them."

I couldn't believe it. "What?"

"You like everyone wanting to be *your* friend, but you don't like it happening to *me*."

I almost never lose my temper, but that made me REALLY angry. "That is so not true!"

"It is!" We'd reached her mum's wedding

dress shop. She swung around and marched inside.

I stared after her. How dare she say that? I wasn't jealous of her being liked. I *wanted* her to be liked, but I wanted her to be liked for being her, with all *her* likes and dislikes, not for being this fake new Mia she was pretending to be.

I let out an angry sigh and carried on to the bakery. Hopefully, by the morning, she would realise just how stupid she was being!

THINGS NOT TO DO WHEN YOU
ARE TRYING TO MAKE FRIENDS

· Copy people all the time
· Pretend to be into things you aren't into
· Laugh really loudly
· Agree all the time
· Say stuff you don't mean!!

10

I wondered if Mia would call for me before
school. After our row, I wasn't surprised
when I got a text.

Mum's giving me a lift today. See u at schl.

That was all it said. No kisses or anything.
Luckily, Alice had also texted me to say she
was at her gran's and could we walk to school
together.

"Where's Mia?" she said, when I knocked
on Mrs Rees's door and fought off the tidal
wave of eager-to-say-hello pugs. "Is she ill?"

"No," I said.

Alice frowned. She shut the dogs inside and
called a goodbye to her gran. "Have you two

had a row?" she asked as we set off.

I nodded.

"Was it about what she said about Baking Club?"

I nodded. "We had an argument on the way home."

Alice shook her head. "I'm not surprised. I couldn't believe she said that. She *doesn't* think Baking Club is boring. She loves baking as much as you do."

"Yes, but *Misha* thinks Baking Club is lame, so of course Mia has to agree with her . . ." I stopped. I might be feeling cross with Mia, but I didn't want to start saying horrible things about her. We'd had a row but she was still my best friend. Well, at least I hoped she was.

Alice gave me a sympathetic look and changed the subject. "I'm having my hair done tonight. I hope it looks good."

"It'll look great," I said. "You're so lucky you're allowed. What else are you getting for your birthday?"

We chatted all the way to school. When we got there, Mia was standing by the lockers with Misha and Lara. She was laughing at something Misha had said. Seeing me, she stopped and gave me a wary look.

I took a breath. I really didn't want us to not be speaking, so I forced myself to make an effort. "Hi."

"Hi," she said.

I started unpacking my bag. I took out the two recipes for cake bases I'd written up and printed out the night before. "These are some recipes I've done for the article," I told Mia. "Have you done any yet?"

"Oh." She looked uncomfortable. "Um . . . not yet. I'll do them soon."

I nodded. "OK. We probably should get on with writing it."

"Yeah."

I hesitated, then turned away. The memory of our argument was like an invisible barrier between us. I fiddled with some books in my locker so I didn't have to talk to her. For once, I was really glad when the bell went and it was time for lessons to begin.

The rest of the day was strange. Mia and I

were kind of talking but we also weren't.

When school was over, we walked to the bakery in silence. I wondered whether to bring up the magazine article but decided not to. *She* should be the one to make the effort.

We came to the street the bakery was on. "I . . . um . . . can't come to the bakery today," she said. "Mum asked me to meet her."

"Oh." I was taken aback. She hadn't mentioned it before.

"I'll see you tomorrow." She hurried away.

I'd hoped that maybe we'd make up before school tomorrow. Now that didn't look likely to happen.

When I got to the bakery, Paula, Mum and Dylan all wanted to know where Mia was. "She's busy tonight," I said, not wanting to admit we'd had a row. Luckily, the shop was busy, so I was able to throw myself into helping and no one asked anything more.

George arrived with his mum on his way to tennis training. He came over to chat, until Sarah tapped him on the shoulder.

"Come on, George, we haven't got time to stand around."

George frowned. "Five minutes won't make a difference, Mum."

"Five minutes' practice could be the difference between winning and losing in your tournament at the weekend," Sarah told him. "What if your opponents have done five minutes more practice every day?"

George scowled and rolled his eyes at me. He said goodbye and left. I watched him go. He obviously hadn't talked to his mum about any of the stuff he'd told me. I wondered whether he would.

Next day, Alice came into school with her new hair. Mia kept on and on about how brilliant it looked until I think Alice almost began to wish she hadn't had it dip-dyed at all. Mia also had a new phone case to show off. It was identical to Lara's. From the expression on Lara's face, I could tell she wasn't pleased Mia had bought exactly the same one, but she didn't say anything.

Mia and I hardly spoke for the rest of the day, and when school finished she said she had to meet her mum again so she didn't come to the bakery. I really missed her. I wanted things to be right between us but I didn't see why I should be the one to make the first move. And Mia didn't seem to want to either. She seemed happy enough – laughing at Misha's jokes and talking about music. She had even started talking about ponies and how much she'd like to start riding.

It was so frustrating. Why couldn't she just be herself?

I wondered if Baking Club on Thursday would change things. If we were baking together, I couldn't imagine us not relaxing and chatting happily. I hoped I was right.

When the bell rang for lunch, I hurried to the lockers to meet Mia. My tummy fluttered with anticipation.

"Time for you two to go and do your

loser thing," said Misha, grinning.

"Yep," I said. "Are you ready?" I asked Mia.

"It's such a shame, Mia. You were almost becoming cool this week. Now you have to go and spoil it," Misha said.

Mia hesitated.

"Come on," I said to her.

"I . . ." She took a deep breath and then the words burst out of her. "I'm not coming, Hannah."

My mouth fell open. "What? Why?"

Alice frowned. "Yes, why not, Mia?"

Mia shook her head. "I just don't want to. It's boring."

"Mia, don't be stupid," Misha said. She looked taken aback. "I wasn't being serious. Go to Baking Club with Hannah."

Mia shook her head. "No."

Tears prickled at my eyes. Maybe I should have suspected that Mia would pull out, after the way she'd been acting all week, but I'd never really thought she would. I swung round and marched away before anyone could see how upset I was.

"Hannah!" I heard Alice call, but I didn't stop.

By the time I reached Baking Club, I felt slightly calmer, but still miserable. It was official. Mia, my best friend, had disappeared.

At least the baking helped take my mind off things. A bit, anyway. Miss Harris started the session by talking about the different kinds of things that could be made out of puff pastry and then sent us off to work in pairs. Luckily, there was a Year 8 girl who didn't have a partner because her friend was ill. She was called Danni and she was really nice. But what would I do next week when her friend came back? Go with Miss Harris, I guess, I thought gloomily.

Miss Harris had brought pastry for us to use because it was really difficult to make. We just had to roll it out and make the sausagemeat filling, then form the sausage rolls.

"Where's Mia this week, Hannah?" Miss Harris asked, as I rolled out the pastry.

"She . . . she couldn't come," I said.

I hoped Miss Harris wouldn't ask why. I didn't want to have to explain it in case I started to cry but, to my relief, she didn't. Instead she said, "How's the article going? Have you decided what it's going to be about yet?"

"Yes – it's going to be on special occasion cakes; how to make them and decorate them." I swallowed hard, feeling my cheeks flush. If Mia wasn't doing Baking Club any more, then she wouldn't want to do the article with me either. It would be too 'boring' for her.

"That sounds perfect," Miss Harris said. "Will it be ready in two weeks' time?"

I nodded.

Miss Harris moved on. I pushed thoughts of Mia away and concentrated on what I was doing. As I smoothed the sausagemeat and rolled up the pastry, I started to feel better. Danni was nice. She asked about the bakery and what I liked to bake. By the time Baking Club had finished and we were packing the still-warm sausage rolls into our tins, I felt, if not exactly happy, then *happier*.

When I got back to the classroom, the others were sitting doing their homework.

Misha saw me first. "Hey! You're back!" she said, jumping to her feet. "How was it?"

I knew that she was feeling bad about what had happened. I was sure she'd never meant her teasing to make Mia to back out of Baking Club. "It was good," I said. "We made sausage rolls."

"Yum!" said Alice. "Do we get to try them?"

"Of course." I opened the tin.

Lara took a deep breath. "Mmm, they smell delicious, Hannah. I wish I could bake like you."

The three of them were being so nice. It made it even more obvious that Mia wasn't saying anything. I glanced at her. Her eyes darted away and she blushed.

Misha, Alice and Lara each took a sausage roll. I offered the tin to Mia. "Do  you want one?" I asked stiffly.

"No, thanks," she muttered.

There was an uncomfortable

silence and then thankfully the end-of-lunch bell went. Mia jumped up, mumbled goodbye and hurried back to her own classroom. The rest of us sat down in our places for registration. Alice glanced at me. "I'm sorry about Mia not going to Baking Club," she whispered. "Misha was really quiet all lunchtime. I think she feels bad for teasing Mia. She never expected her not to go to Baking Club."

I bit my lip. "That makes two of us."

"What will you do?" said Alice. "Have you got to write that article on your own now?"

"Yeah, but I don't mind. I can do it at the weekend and take some photos of me making a cake."

"I could help, if you like," said Alice.

Alice knows about as much about baking as I know about ponies. It was lovely of her to offer, though. "Thanks. It's OK though. I'll manage."

I smiled at her but I felt a flicker of sadness. It wouldn't be anything like so much fun doing it all without Mia.

After school, I walked back to the bakery alone again. Mia and I were officially not talking now.

Paula frowned when I came in. "No Mia again today?"

"No," I said shortly.

"Have you two had a row?" she said, peering at me.

I nodded and felt myself tense. If she told me it was in the stars I thought I might walk straight out again. But she just came round the counter to give me a hug. "Oh, you poor thing. Was it a bad one?"

I nodded.

Mum came through from the kitchen then and saw Paula hugging me, so I had to tell her what had happened too, and Dylan overheard. They were all really nice.

Mum kissed me. "You can always go home, sweetie, if you don't feel like helping today."

But I didn't want to go home to an empty house. I'd far rather be in the warm, comforting atmosphere of the bakery.

"You'll make up with Mia," Paula said. "You'll be friends again soon."

I wished I could believe her, but that would only happen if Mia admitted she was wrong and stopped trying to pretend to be something she wasn't. And was that going to happen any time soon?

I didn't think so.

TYPES OF PASTRY

SWEET SHORTCRUST PASTRY - perfect
  for fruit pies

SHORTCRUST PASTRY - perfect for
  savoury pies and quiches

PUFF PASTRY - perfect for sausage rolls, savoury
  tarts, cream cakes and fruit turnovers

CHOUX PASTRY - light and airy and perfect for
  profiteroles and éclairs

11

Mia and I didn't speak to each other at all on Friday. We still hung around with Misha, Lara and Alice, but it's fairly easy to avoid talking to someone directly if you're in a group.

On the way back from school, I spotted Mia walking slowly ahead of me towards her mum's shop, her shoulders hunched, head down. She'd been quieter when she was with the others too, listening rather than joining in. Occasionally I would catch her looking at me. I wondered if she was missing me as much as I was missing her.

That evening, I distracted myself by starting to write the article.

I soon had two pages roughly planned out, and I'd decided on the title:

'SO, YOU WANT TO BAKE A SPECIAL CAKE?'

Underneath I'd written two recipes – one for a chocolate sponge and one for a carrot cake. There was a section I hadn't filled in yet which was going to be about icing. In a box to one side there was a bit about Mum and the bakery. There were photos of some of Mum's cakes, including the wedding cake and George's cake, and some of the display cakes from the shop. It looked OK, but I wasn't completely happy. I wanted it to really stand out and grab people's attention so they would read it. At the moment it just didn't do that.

I sighed. I decided to think about it some more over the weekend and maybe have another go. I saved the file and then got out my maths homework.

My phone buzzed.

To my surprise it was a text from George:

Wuu2?

Nothing much. U?

Night off tennis! My mates are over with their guitars. It's awesome! Lol

I replied:

☺

George texted again: Alec wants us 2 all start a band.

R u going 2?

Can't. 2 much tennis. L

U shd tell ur mum how u feel.

No.

U SHOULD.

I waited for his reply. At last it came.

Maybe.

Did he mean it?

DO IT! I texted.

He didn't reply to that. I waited, but nothing came through. I sighed. I couldn't wait forever. I really should get on with my maths.

Just before bed, I got another text from George.

Told Mum. It didn't go well.

Why?

Apparently I'm just having 'a wobble' and I can't stop, not after so much time and money, blah blah blah.

I could hear the bitterness in his text.

☹ Really sorry.

Thx. See u soon.

Yeah. See u.

I pressed Send and flopped back on my bed. Poor George. Poor me. Life felt pretty rubbish right now.

There was a knock on the door. Mum came in with a mug of hot chocolate. "I thought you might like this," she said.

I smiled at her and sat up. "Thanks." She'd even put whipped cream on the top and sprinkled it with grated chocolate.

I sipped it as she sat down beside me.

"So, what *is* going on with you and Mia?" she asked.

I sighed and told her the full story about Mia not wanting to come to Baking Club any more. I didn't leave anything out.

"Oh dear," Mum said, shaking her head. "I

can see she just wants to fit in, but pretending to be someone she's not isn't going to make her happy. You have to be who you want to be, not who other people expect you to be."

"I know. It's like . . ." I paused, trying to think of the right way to phrase it. "It's like a choux bun trying to be a shortcrust pastry," I said finally.

Mum smiled. "Yep, though I don't think many people would get the comparison."

Mia would, I thought. And suddenly I missed her more than ever.

"I don't know what to do," I said.

Mum stroked my hair. "You could try making up with her."

"But why should I be the one to make the first move? I haven't done anything wrong. *I'm* not the one who's changed."

"I know, sweetie," Mum said softly. "But sometimes it's best not to think about things like that. You need to concentrate on finding a way to be happy again – and that means you might have to be the one who tries to be friends again."

I knew Mum was right. I sipped the hot chocolate for a moment. A thought struck me. "Even if I do go and see her and try to make up, it's not going to make any difference, not until she decides to stop pretending she's into music and make-up and that she doesn't like baking."

Mum nodded. "I suppose that's true. But maybe you can help her realise she'll be much happier if she accepts she's a choux bun." We looked at each other and suddenly giggled. I felt a bit better.

Mum kissed my head. "Finish your hot chocolate and then it's bedtime. OK?"

"OK," I said. "Thanks."

It was very strange not having Mia at the bakery the next day – Saturday. Dylan had brought in some of his homemade meat pies to show Mum. They were delicious, and I wished Mia could have tried them too. I even took a photo of Dylan holding them before realising I couldn't exactly send it to her now that we weren't talking.

The door bell tinkled and George came in with his mum. I fixed a smile on my face as he came over to buy his usual two sausage rolls.

"How's it going?" I asked, as our mums started chatting, arranging to meet for a coffee the next afternoon.

"Oh . . . you know," he said, sighing. "Tennis and more tennis. I've got a big match tomorrow."

He didn't seem angry or annoyed, just really down. "Can't you talk to your mum again?" I whispered.

"What's the point? She won't listen." He shook his head. "Nah, it's easier just to get on with it."

I frowned. "There must be something you can do."

"There isn't," he said bleakly.

"We'd better go, George," Sarah called.

"Good luck tomorrow," I said.

"Thanks," he muttered.

Paula watched him go. "Taurus," she said, checking her newspaper. "That's what he is. Ah ha! Here we go. 'Financial strain is weighing heavily on you, but change is afoot. Mars is now rising and it's time to take the bull by its horns, to look to the future, not the past.'"

She nodded wisely. "He should take note."

"I don't think George has financial problems," I said.

"The stars often speak in mysterious ways," Paula said, tapping her nose. "Mars is rising."

I had a sudden vision of a Mars bar rising into the stars and I wanted so much for Mia to be there, so we could roll our eyes at each other. But then I remembered that, even if she were there, she wouldn't be the old Mia. She'd changed so much.

I wished I could wave a magic wand and change her back.

12

When we got back home that afternoon, I tried to finish off the magazine article. It was fun but, just like at the bakery, I missed sharing it with Mia.

I looked at my phone. I thought about what Mum had said about it not being important to be right, and making the first move. Before I could change my mind, I sent Mia a text.

Wuu2?

I put my phone down and went back to my article.

Suddenly my phone buzzed. It was Mia.

Nothing much. How abt u? How was the bakery 2day?

I was pleased. She'd replied *and* she'd asked a question. She obviously wanted me to text her back.

Good, I typed. I hesitated and then added: I missed u tho ☹.

The reply came almost immediately.

Missed u 2 ☹ ☹. I was just at Mum's shop. Wuu2 now?

My heart leapt.

Writing the article for the mag.

I wondered what she would say. There was a longer pause this time.

Bet it's brilliant. xxx

I stared at my phone, not knowing what to say. Then she texted again: Gotta go. Thx for txting. xxx

I replied: xxx.

I smiled to myself. I know a few texts isn't much, but it felt good to have at least made contact. I wasn't sure how we would do it, but maybe, just maybe, we could be friends again after all . . .

"Teenagers are so difficult," Sarah said. She was sitting having a coffee with Mum in our kitchen on Sunday afternoon while George was at his tennis tournament. I was measuring the ingredients to make a chocolate cake for Alice's birthday. I was planning to take it into school the next day. Mark was out at a birthday party with the twins.

"Hannah's not too bad," Mum said, throwing a smile at me. "But maybe that will all change when she reaches her teens."

"I sometimes feel like I just don't understand George," Sarah said, cradling her coffee in her hands. "Our life revolves around letting him do what he loves, and yet he can be so moody. I don't expect undying gratitude, but it would be nice if he at least seemed happy when we go to tennis."

I frowned. Now George had talked to her about the tennis, surely she'd have realised that was the reason he was often grumpy.

"And over the last few days he's just gone really quiet," Sarah said. "I don't know what's the matter with him. He's barely speaking at all and we had this strange conversation the other day where he tried to convince me he didn't like tennis any more."

"What happened?" Mum asked Sarah.

"Well, I was stumped at first. He loves tennis, always has done, it's been his life since he was three. Then I remembered something that Bill, his coach, once told me about how kids often have a wobble in confidence at about this age. All the pressure and practice get too much and some kids say they don't want to play any more. Bill says they don't mean it, and as a parent you need to be strong and tell them to stick with it and they'll soon start enjoying it again." She sighed. "It's hard. I hate being a pushy mum, but he's so talented. Quitting tennis isn't going to make him happy."

So that was why she hadn't listened to George – she didn't believe him!

Sarah was shaking her head. "I really don't know what to do with him. Hopefully, if he wins his match today he'll settle down again."

"So why aren't you there?" Mum asked.

"Oh, I'll go along later. He's not playing until 4 o'clock. It's best if I stay out of the way while he prepares."

I longed to tell her how George felt about tennis. But it was none of my business. It had to be George who did that. Maybe I'd text him later.

I finished measuring out the cake ingredients.

Sarah watched. "Baking reminds me of making beauty products. All the measuring and mixing and the magic of watching the ingredients transform into something else – something wonderful."

135

"I love that magic," said Mum. "Are you going to take a photo of this cake for the article?"

"I'll see how it turns out," I said.

"What article are you doing?" Sarah asked.

I explained. "I want to make it really eye-catching so people want to try baking for themselves. Or even decide to order one of Mum's cakes!"

"When you're selling beauty products, it always helps to have a model with them," Sarah said. "Someone who shows how beautiful you might look if you use the product."

Mum grinned. "I'm not sure that would work with cakes."

Just then there was a ringing from the kitchen table. It was my phone. I checked the number. Mia!

I wiped my hands and answered. "Hi."

"Hannah!" Mia's voice rose in a wail. "You HAVE to help me! I don't know who else to call."

"Why? What's going on?" I asked. She sounded really upset.

Mia gave a couple of strangled sobs. "My hair, Hannah! I tried to dye my hair."

"You didn't!" I gasped. "What happened?"

"Oh, Hannah! It's a disaster. When my mum sees, she is going to freak. There's no way I can go into school looking like this! Please help me – please!"

Mum came over. "Is everything OK?" she mouthed.

I shook my head and covered the phone. "Mia's dyed her hair and it's gone wrong."

"Oh no," Mum said, her eyes widening.

Sarah appeared behind Mum. "Tell her to come round. Maybe I can do something to help."

I remembered that she had said she had once worked at a hairdresser's. "Mia, come round. George's mum is here and she might be able to help."

Mia was snuffling at the end of the phone. "I don't think anyone can sort my hair out."

"Just come round," I told her.

"OK."

I clicked the phone off and looked at Mum and Sarah. "She sounds terrible."

"Poor Mia. I wonder how bad her hair is," said Mum.

The answer was VERY bad indeed. When Mia turned up on the doorstep, she was wearing a hat. (I also noticed she had a bag *exactly* like Misha's new bag, but I decided not to ask about it right then. There were other, more important, things to deal with.)

"Well?" I said, pulling her inside and leading her through to the kitchen. "Let's see."

Slowly, Mia removed her hat. My hand flew to my mouth and I gasped. Mum and Sarah did the same.

"Oh dear," said Mum faintly.

"Mia, what have you done?" I breathed.

The ends of Mia's strawberry blonde hair were now frizzy and a straw-like yellow.

"I tried to dip-dye it blonde," she said, her eyes filling with tears. "But I didn't bother doing a strand test like the pack said and I didn't time it properly. When I took it off, this  was what it looked like." She burst into tears. "What am I going to do?"

She looked completely devastated. Mum and I rushed to hug her.

"Don't panic," said Sarah, coming over and looking at Mia's hair closely. "It's not all of your hair – that's the most important thing, it's just the ends. I can definitely do something with this."

"You can get it back to normal?" Mia said hopefully.

"I can't do that," said Sarah. "The ends are too badly damaged to dye back, but I could cut it and make it look better."

"No!" gasped Mia. "I don't want it cut. I've been growing it for ages."

"It's the only way, I'm afraid," said Sarah. "Unless you want to go to school looking like this?"

Mia swallowed. "OK."

"I'll have to speak to your mum first and check it's OK," said Sarah. "Does she know you dyed it?"

"No," Mia whispered. "She's visiting my gran. I was at home with my dad."

"Oh, Mia," said Mum shaking her head. "Come on, let's give her a ring."

A little while later, Mia was sitting in a chair in the kitchen with wet hair and a towel around her shoulders. Sarah picked up sections of her hair one at a time and cut them. She'd described to Mia a hairstyle she thought would work with her hair and face shape. Mia had just nodded miserably.

I finished Alice's cake while Sarah worked.

"OK, I've got rid of the damaged ends," she said. "I think it would do your hair good to have a conditioning treatment, as well. Let's see." She looked around the kitchen. "We could make one up. Rose, I don't suppose you have any avocados?"

"We have a couple in the fridge," Mum said. "I was going to make a salad with them."

"Could we use them? I'll also need some olive oil and an egg yolk."

"OK," Mum said.

Mia and I watched as Sarah mashed an avocado with an egg yolk and a teaspoon of olive oil. "All these ingredients are really good for conditioning and moisturising hair," she explained. "I'd usually put a few drops of lavender or rosemary essential oil in to make it smell nice too."

"I've got lavender oil upstairs," Mum said. She hurried to get it.

Sarah mixed everything into a thick green paste and then started to smooth it onto Mia's hair, covering the ends.

I had to bite my cheeks to stop myself from giggling. Mia looked very strange with green gloop on her head.

"Now sit there for ten minutes," Sarah told her.

Mum and Sarah went to have a cup of tea.

"I feel silly," Mia said glumly.

"You look a bit silly," I said, grinning. "Shall I take a photo?"

"Don't you dare!" she said.

We smiled at each other and I felt a sudden happy glow. It was really nice having her round at my house – even if it was for such a horrible reason. I'd missed her.

"Why did you try to dip-dye your hair?" I asked. "Your hair was great as it was."

Mia sighed. "Alice's hair looks so good, and I wanted mine to look the same."

"But Alice's hair is really different to yours," I said.

"I know," she said miserably. "I just thought it would look OK."

"You have to think about what would suit *you*," I told her. "Not what looks good on someone else. You need to be yourself, not just copy people."

Mia's eyes flicked to the bag on the floor; the one that was identical to Misha's.

I remembered what Mum and I had been saying the other day. "OK, it's kind of like . . . if you're a choux bun, you should just be happy being a choux bun."

She looked confused. "What?"

"You shouldn't try to be a shortcrust pastry."

Her lips twitched.

"Do you get it?" I said.

She couldn't hold back her smile. "I do, but you're officially weird, Hannah. You do know that?"

I smiled. "Yep."

She sighed and rubbed her forehead. "I guess I just want Misha, Alice and Lara to like me, and I thought if I was more like them then they would."

"I know, and that works a bit, but you don't have to be exactly the same as them," I said. "In fact, I think if you take that bag

into school Misha might not like you at all."
I looked at the bag again. "Why did you get
it?"

Mia blushed. "Well, Misha laughed at my
cupcake one so I thought if I got one just like
hers it would be better."

She really was clueless. "But Misha wants
to be the only one of us who has a bag like
that, Mia. She'll be really mad if you go into
school with it."

"Oh." Mia bit her lip. "Maybe I'd better
ask Mum to take it back."

"I think you should. Also, it's a
Misha kind of bag. It doesn't suit
you. The cupcakes one does,
though – I really like it. Do you
like it?"

She nodded.

"Then that's the one you should have."

Our eyes met. "Thanks, Hannah," she said.
"I'm . . . I'm really sorry I dropped out of
Baking Club and left you to do the article on
your own."

"I haven't finished it yet," I said.

Mia gave me a hopeful look. "Would you still like some help with it?"

"Yes! Although . . ." I said. "Only people who come to Baking Club can write a Baking Club article."

"So, you mean I'd have to come back to Baking Club," said Mia.

I nodded.

Mia grinned. "It's a deal!"

I high-fived her. "And if anyone tries to laugh at you, I'll just tell them you're a choux bun!"

We both giggled.

Sarah and Mum came back in. Mum caught my eye and smiled. I grinned back.

"Time to go upstairs and take this off," said Sarah to Mia. "Dry your hair and then you can see your new hairstyle."

I held up crossed fingers as Mia stood up and went to the bathroom with Sarah.

Mum came and put her arm round me. "You and Mia look as if you've made up."

"Yes," I said happily. "We have."

MIA'S HAIR CONDITIONING TREATMENT

Ingredients:

Half an avocado

1 egg yolk

A teaspoon of olive oil

2 drops of lavender or rosemary oil

What to do:

Mash the avocado with a fork and then mix the other ingredients in. Mix until it becomes a smooth, thick paste. Put on to clean damp hair (after shampooing and rinsing), putting most on to the ends of the hair. Then wait for at least ten minutes before washing off.

Result:

super-smooth and shiny hair!

Top tip: Cover hair with a shower cap while the mixture is soaking in so it doesn't drip everywhere.

Mia's new hairstyle looked A-MA-ZING!
Sarah had cut it into choppy layers with
a side-swept fringe, and the conditioning
treatment had left her hair shiny and glossy.

"Oh, wow!" I said.

Mia was beaming from ear to ear. "I love it!
It's so much nicer than it was before. Thank
you!"

"You're a miracle worker," Mum said to
Sarah.

"I enjoyed it. It's ages since I've done
any hairdressing. It was fun making the
conditioner too, and it seems to have
worked."

Mia touched her hair. "It's so soft and
shiny."

"Well, I'd better be going," said Sarah. "See you all soon."

"Say hi to George for me," I said.

"I hope he does well in his competition," said Mum.

Sarah left, and Mia and I set about decorating Alice's birthday cake. I decided to use Mum's tennis cake idea as inspiration. We covered it with a chocolate ganache then put a rectangle of green fondant icing on top.

Only, it wasn't a tennis court – we made it into a horse-jumping arena. We made jumps out of candy canes and borrowed three of Molly's little plastic model horses and put them near the jumps. Then I wrote "Happy Birthday" on a piece of

white fondant icing that Mia cut out to look like a trophy and stuck on the side of the cake. It looked brilliant.

Mum came in to look at it. "That's wonderful!" she said. "You have to take a picture!"

We took a photo and then helped clear away.

"I'm going to make some soup and bread for dinner in a little while," said Mum. "Do you two want to help with the bread?"

"Definitely," I said, looking at Mia, who nodded. "Call us when you're ready to start."

Mia and I went to the computer to work on the Baking Club article. Mia added a Victoria sponge recipe and we finished the icing section together.

"It's missing something," said Mia, looking at it critically. "I wish we could make it even more eye-catching."

"I know," I said. It looked good, but would it make people stop and read it?

What could we do?

Just then Mum came upstairs. She was

on the phone and she was looking worried. "Hannah, you haven't heard from George this afternoon, have you?"

"No." I checked my phone just to be sure, but there were no texts from him. "Why?"

Mum shook her head at me and went back to the phone. "Sorry, Sarah, Hannah's not heard from him. I'll let you know if he does get in touch. Call me if there's any news." She clicked the phone off.

"What's happening?" I said.

"It's George," Mum said. "He's disappeared."

13

Apparently George had disappeared just before his tennis match. The coach had left him getting changed and, when he'd come back, George was gone. Sarah had tried all his tennis friends and friends from school, but none of them had seen him.

"Sarah's really worried," Mum said. "Why would he have just got up and left?"

I bit my lip. I'd wanted to keep George's secret but, right now, I couldn't. "I think I know," I said.

"What do you mean? Hannah, this is serious. If you know something, you have to tell me."

"Well, he was talking about it the other day

at the bakery. He's fed up of playing tennis. He hates all the training he has to do. He tried to talk to his mum on Thursday but she didn't listen."

Mum bit her lip. "Oh, goodness. Sarah said he'd not been himself the last few days. Was that why?"

I nodded.

Mum shook her head. "I'd better ring Sarah and tell her what you've just told me."

I nodded. Mum left the room.

"Poor George," said Mia.

"I know. He didn't want to talk to his mum, then when he finally did, she turned round and said she'd spent too much money on lessons and stuff for him to just give it up. I thought she was really mean, but when she was here today she told Mum about it – she said she thought he was just having a bit of a wobble and she was trying to be supportive."

"He really meant it, though?"

I nodded. "I wonder where he is."

Mum came back in. "I've spoken to Sarah.

If he does text you or phone you, can you tell me? He's not answering his phone."

"OK." I hoped he was all right and not doing anything stupid. Where would he go?

Suddenly my phone buzzed. I checked the screen.

R u at home?

George! It was a message from George!
"Mia – look!" I said.
I quickly texted back.

Yep, I'm here. Where r u?

Walking around. Can I come over?

YES!

I decided not to say anything about people looking for him or being worried. I texted again.

See u soon. ☺

"Mum!" I shouted. "Mum! George has texted. He's coming here!"

Five minutes later there was a knock on the door. I flung it open and saw George on the doorstep. "Where have you been?" I said. I was so relieved to see him, I even gave him a hug. "Come in. Your mum's on her way over."

George frowned. "She knows I'm here?"

"Yes. She's been worried sick," my mum said, coming into the hall. "We had to tell her. What happened, George? Where have you been?"

"I left the sports centre and got a bus back to town," he said.

"Why?"

He rubbed his eyes. "I just couldn't do it." He came in and I shut the door behind him. "I couldn't face one more match – so I just left. I know Mum will be really upset, but I just don't think I want to play tennis any more."

"Oh, George," Mum said.

"I tried to tell her, but she wouldn't listen."

"She'll be here soon; you can talk to her yourself," said Mum. "Don't worry. I'm sure she'll understand."

George didn't look so sure.

I took him through to the kitchen to distract him.

"Hi," Mia said. She had been measuring ingredients to make the bread. "We were just about to make some bread. Do you want to help?"

He smiled. "OK. I'll have a go."

I pulled out a chair for him.

We mixed the flour, yeast, salt and sugar together and made the dough. We'd made enough for three loaves – one for each of us. Mia and I showed George how to knead his dough – pushing and rolling it and slapping it down on the table. He got really into it.

"I like this," he said.

"The more you can knead it, the better," I said. "Because the more you stretch and pull it, the stronger it gets."

As we were working, Mum got up and went into the hall.

"There!" Mia said at last. "I think mine's done."

"Mine too," I agreed. My dough was smooth and elastic and I formed it into a round.

George showed us his. "Perfect," I told him.

"Do we cook them now?" he said.

"Not yet. You've got to cover it and leave it to prove," I said.

"Prove what?" asked George, puzzled.

"'Prove' means leaving it so the yeast can start to work and the dough rise," explained Mia. "It'll double in size and then we knock the air out of it and leave it again for at least another half an hour before we bake it."

"That's ages," said George.

"It's worth it, though," I said. "Fresh bread is the best thing in the world."

"I second that," a voice said from the doorway.

We all looked round. Sarah was standing there with Mum. We'd been so engrossed that I wasn't sure how long she had been there, watching us.

"Mum!" George said.

She came forward. "George, I've been so worried. How could you just leave like that?"

He shot me a look. I nodded encouragingly. I knew he had to talk to her.

"I can't do it any more, Mum," he said. "I don't want to spend all my spare time practising and miss out on other stuff. I don't care about the competitions and tournaments."

"But you're so good at tennis," his mum said.

"I know, but I just need a break."

"Do you really mean that?" Sarah said quietly.

"Yes," he said, hanging his head. "I'm sorry, Mum."

She sighed. "I had no idea. You should have told me sooner. I only encouraged you to play because I thought it made you happy. If it's making you miserable, then of course you can stop. It'll be strange." She managed a smile. "But it's the right thing to do."

I saw the relief on George's face.

Sarah gave a small laugh and looked at Mum. "I don't know what we'll do with all our free time. It's been tennis, tennis, tennis for the last nine years."

"I'm going to hang out with friends and play the drums," said George. "Maybe we can start a band after all."

Mum looked at Sarah. "And there's a little shop near the bakery that's empty."

Sarah's eyes met hers. "I couldn't," she said doubtfully.

"I did," Mum told her.

"Don't just dream it – do it," I said. "And, just think, if you start your own beauty business, George could be one of your models," I added, nudging him.

"No way!" George said.

"Really?" said Mia. "I can see you advertising face creams."

"Or hair conditioner," I said.

"Perfume?" said Mia.

We grinned at each other, and George glared at us.

Mum and Sarah chuckled. "You know," Mum said to Sarah, "Stopping tennis might be a good thing for you and George."

Sarah smiled. "You might be right."

14

George and his mum took his share of the bread dough home with them after Mia and I had given them instructions on how to bake it.

George texted me that evening:

Bread was AWESOME! Thx. I mean it. ☺

I smiled. I had a feeling he was thanking me for more than just the bread.

Mia and I finished the article and showed it to Mum. She suggested that she make a couple of new cakes so we could have photos of those as well.

"I want a few more cakes to display in the

shop anyway," she said. "You can help me make them next weekend if you both want."

"Oh yes!" we said together.

It was so brilliant having Mia back to being Mia again. I went to sleep very happy that night.

"OMG, Mia! Your hair!" exclaimed Misha on Monday morning. "It looks great!"

"Thanks," Mia said. Her hair did look really good with its different length layers and long side fringe.

"I didn't even know you were getting it cut," said Lara.

Mia grinned at me. "Neither did I."

We'd decided not to say anything about the dip-dye disaster. That would be our secret.

"We've got some news. Mia's coming back to Baking Club," I said.

"Really?" said Misha.

Mia took a breath. "Yep."

Misha grinned. "Awesome. That means

we get twice as many cakes and biscuits to eat."

"Only if you're nice to us," Mia said to her. "What do you think, Hannah?"

"Oh, she has to be VERY nice," I teased. "Oh, and I just remembered, this is for you!" I said to Alice, showing her a photo of her birthday cake on my phone. "Mia and I made it. Mum's going to drop it off at your gran's today. We wanted to bring it to school but she said it would get ruined."

"It's amazing!" Alice said, beaming. "Thank you so much! You all have to come round and help me eat it."

"Let's see," said Misha. She took the phone and looked at the photos. "Hey, you've got loads of photos of cakes here, Hannah."

"I know. They're for the article," I said.

"Mmmm, I like *this* one!" Misha said.

I saw that she was looking at the photo of George standing by his cake.

"He looks VERY cute in this," said Misha. She flicked on. "Oh, wow. This one's even better."

She held up the picture I'd taken of Dylan holding the meat pies.

"That's not a cake," I said.

"Who cares?" said Misha. "I'd come into the bakery to buy *anything* from him."

My heart did a double flip. Of course! That was it! Sarah had said that models in photographs attracted customers. Well, maybe photos of cute boys standing by the cakes would attract girls. At the very least they'd grab their attention and get them looking at the article!

"That's it!" I gasped. "I know what this article needs!"

"What?" asked Alice.

I grinned. "Just wait and see!"

The article was a massive success. And I mean MASSIVE. I followed up my idea and asked Dylan and George to bring some of their friends to the bakery. Mia and I helped Mum make some new cakes and they

posed alongside them. As well as the original photo of George with his tennis cake, there was a photo of a guitar-shaped cake with George's friends, Alec and Callum, beside it with their guitars. There was a massive chocolate cake that Dylan was showing off, and a very cute friend of his called Max posing in his swimming trunks beside a cake that looked like a swimming pool with a diving board. That photo really made Misha squeal!

Mum displayed the cakes at the bakery afterwards. Mia pointed out that not everyone would want to look at cute boys, so we also made a pink princess cake and got the twins to stand beside it wearing princess dresses and holding hands. (Ella had to be bribed into wearing her dress!) And, finally, there was a cake in the shape of a bone with three sugar pug dogs on. Mrs Rees's dogs posed for that. I managed to get the photo just before they started to eat the topping. That cake DIDN'T end up in the bakery!

Miss Harris seemed a little surprised when we showed her the article, but when the magazine was printed, people's reactions were awesome. Everyone wanted to know about the bakery.

Mum loved the pictures so much, she asked Mark to make them into an advertising brochure – and then we had an amazing stroke of luck. It turned out that Dylan's friend Max's dad worked for the news department of our local TV station. When Max showed him the copy of the magazine, he asked to interview us and we ended up on TV!

"I can't believe how busy we're going to be," Mum said. "I've had so many orders!"

It was the following Sunday morning and

Mia, Sarah, Mum, Mark and I were all sitting around our kitchen table. Mum, Mark and Sarah were drinking coffee, and Mia and I had hot chocolate. George was otherwise occupied, chasing the twins around the lounge and pretending to be a monster. He's like a different person now – always in a good mood, with a constant smile on his face now he isn't playing tennis competitively.

In the centre of the table was Mum's delicious lemon drizzle cake. I licked my finger and picked up a few stray crumbs. Yum!

"I know you're busy, but you will be able to fit in making a cake for me soon, won't you?" said Sarah. "I've got some news – I've taken out a lease on that empty shop near the bakery. When I'm ready to open my new natural products beauty shop, I want a big cake from the one and only Sugar and Spice Bakery at my launch party."

Mum smiled in delight. "Oh, Sarah! That's wonderful! I'm so pleased."

"It's great news. I can help you set up a website if you like," said Mark.

Sarah's eyes sparkled. "Thank you. I'm spending every second thinking about the products I want to sell – bath bombs, handmade soaps, hair conditioners, body butters. It's *so* much fun. I'm going to sell online too. And maybe have birthday parties in the shop – I thought people might like to know how to make products and take some home with them afterwards. There's a room at the back that would be perfect for that sort of thing."

"We could do parties together!" said Mum. "I could bring cupcakes and they could do cupcake decorating too."

Sarah looked delighted. "Oh yes – that's brilliant!"

Mia and I looked at each other and grinned. They sounded exactly like we did when we got excited about a plan or a project.

"So," Mia said, nudging me. "A cake for a beauty product shop. What do you think?"

"A giant bath bomb?" I suggested.

"Or a tower of cupcakes that look like bath bombs," said Mia.

"A cake in the shape of a tub of body butter?"

"Or a cake decorated with pictures of things the shop sells? Have you got any paper? Let's do some sketches."

I fetched some paper from the sideboard. When I thought about how miserable everyone had been not so long ago – George, Mia, me – I could hardly believe how well things had turned out. I remembered what Mum had said to me once: You have to be who you want to be, not who other people expect you to be. It's so true. If you pretend to be something you're not all the time and keep your true self a secret, it will just make you unhappy.

Mia is completely back to normal now. She even seems able to cope with Misha's teasing. She said to me this morning that she thinks it's like kneading bread. All the pushing and pulling just makes friendships stronger.

I looked around the kitchen and felt a swell of happiness. Family and new friends – talking, laughing, making plans for the future and eating cake. This all started from Mum's dream of having the bakery. I don't know what's in store for us, but I do know it's up to each of us to have our own dreams and try and make them come true.

the orion star

★ ★ ★

CALLING ALL GROWN-UPS!
Sign up for **the orion star** newsletter to
hear about your favourite authors and exclusive
competitions, plus details of how children
can join our 'Story Stars' review panel.

Sign up at:

www.orionbooks.co.uk/orionstar

Follow us 🐦 @the_orionstar
Find us 📘 facebook.com/TheOrionStar